Fallen

Gianna Emiko Barnes

Fulton Books, Inc.
Meadville, PA

Published by Fulton Books 2020

ISBN 978-1-64952-370-9 (paperback)
ISBN 978-1-64952-371-6 (digital)

Printed in the United States of America

Prologue

I can't believe this is happening, Taryn thought to herself as the world seemed to move slower and slower around her in this cold tiny room. Eight years of her life summed up to one simple piece of paper, closing the chapter of what she thought would be her happily ever after, indefinitely. The voices talking to her began to blur, seemingly moving farther away. Forcing a smile on her face, all she could do was nod in a feeble attempt to hold herself together, even if inside she felt as if she were crumbling. How can one physically stay whole when inside so many pieces of themselves are shattering uncontrollably? Everyone in the room began to rise, shake hands as she sat there, frozen. This is it. How did they even get here? Her heartbeat started to pound in her chest, as if trying to break free and run from the room. Her breath, heaving yet shallow, seemed to be slipping from Taryn's control along with the rest of her life, all because of that little piece of paper. "This can't be happening," Taryn repeated to herself in a whisper as she clenched her eyes shut, fighting the tears that threatened to pour down her cheeks. If she could just keep it together, she'd be okay, instead of allowing the pieces of her that was breaking fall away with the rest of the world around her.

Taryn

"Taryn?" Tiana said softly with a gentle touch on the shoulder. "Sweetie, we're here."

Startled and gasping, she shot up in her seat, hands clenching the armrests next to her. Her breath was completely erratic. Looking around the cabin of the airplane, Taryn was forced back to reality. Glancing over at her parents, she couldn't help but smile. Tiana and Noah have been her rocks through everything that life had thrown at her, and every time Taryn had wanted to give up or quit on herself, they refused to let her give up that easily. They didn't raise a quitter, nor did they raise someone who was weak, they'd always remind her when she would find herself fighting through her own darkness.

"We have arrived at the San Francisco International Airport. It is currently 7:36 a.m., with an outside air temperature of fifty-six degrees. We hope you enjoyed your flight with us, and we look forward to servicing you again. Thank you for flying with us. Have a wonderful day," the pilot announced as the plane began to taxi toward the gate.

Relaxing into her chair, Taryn took a deep breath as she tried to blink the nightmare away from her memory. It had been nine months already, yet the memory of that moment had increasingly been haunting her dreams as she got closer and closer to finally opening the next chapter of her life. But this trip was not about her. This weekend would not be about her. It was for Nathan.

As the plane slowed, and the seatbelt-buckle light turned off, the cabin grew with life. People were shifting in their seats, stretching, gathering their belongings, and moving shoulder to shoulder into the aisles. The clicking sounds of the overhead bins were echoing through the plane as they were being opened.

Taking a deep breath, Taryn released the belt buckle and slowly stood up. As her dad began to take their belongings from the overhead bins, Taryn placed them on the empty seat next to hers, making room for her parents to maneuver themselves into the aisle. Once they were settled with their rolling carry-ons, Taryn passed the rest of the belongings back to her parents. As the people in the rows in front of them slowly began to flow forward from the aisles, Taryn glanced back at the empty seat next to hers and sighed heavily before following her parents. Smiling through this weekend alone was going to be much harder than she thought.

"Thank you for flying with us. Enjoy San Francisco," the flight attendants repeated as passengers were herded out the exit of the plane one by one. Taryn moved as if she were in a trance, going with the motions, following the other passengers and her parents down the aisles.

Aisles. *How could something so simple, so taken for granted, bring back such painful memories?* she thought to herself as she stared off toward a path that seemed to take forever to bypass. Never in her life would she consider walking down the aisle a bad thing. It was the happiest moment of her life. Yet walking down this aisle of the plane made her perception of all aisles seem empty, alone, and bleak. Her mind began to wander farther toward her darkness.

As she reached the door of the plane, a rush of cold air smacked Taryn in the face, giving her a wake-up call that she desperately needed to keep her mind from wandering off further. Taking a deep breath and pulling herself back to reality, she smiled at the flight attendants as she stepped off the plane. *Wow. We aren't in Hawaii anymore*, Taryn thought as another burst of wind sent a cold shiver down her spine to the tips of her toes. Just walking down the Jetway, you could feel the fifty-six degrees of coldness just outside the airport walls.

"Taryn, text your brother, and let him know we've landed," Tiana's voice drifted over her shoulder toward Taryn, who fell into pace behind her. "His apartment is forty-five minutes away, so it should give us just enough time to freshen up, brush your teeth, and grab our suitcases from baggage claim." As a dental hygienist before becoming an elementary school teacher, brushing your teeth was definitely always emphasized growing up. But Tiana might be pushing it more so now, as Taryn smelled the tinge of tequila left on her breath as she let out a heavy sigh.

"Yes, Mom," Taryn dragged out, looking to her dad as they both giggled to themselves quietly.

"Nate. Just landed. Mom's making us brush our teeth before we get the bags. Take your time." (Taryn)

"Gotcha. Be there in a few. Lmk when you guys are on the curb with the bags." (Nathan)

As they entered the restroom, Tiana stopped and stared at her daughter for a moment. She knew Taryn would put on a good show for her brother, not wanting her issues to take away from this huge moment in his life, but Tiana was still concerned. Even though Taryn was thirty now, she was still Tiana's baby girl.

"Are you okay, honey?" Tiana asked, trying to mask the depth of concern in her voice. "You know we're here for you, right?"

"Mom," Taryn replied with a sigh. "It's been nine months already. I'm fine." She glanced at her mom in the reflection of the mirror, seeing true worry shadowing the sleep in Tiana's eyes.

Clearly not believing her, Tiana continued to stare at her daughter in the mirror, giving a slight head tilt as she waited for Taryn to give her a bigger sign, or just explain her reaction on the plane a little further.

"Mom, I promise I'm fine," Taryn said with a slight smile as she softened her eyes toward her overly concerned mother.

"Are you sure?"

"Yes, Mom, I'm sure. I'll be fine. It was just a bad dream," Taryn replied, sounding as if she was trying to convince herself more than her mother.

"Promise?"

"I promise, Mom," she said with a heavy sigh and a forced smile. "Besides, even if I wasn't, this weekend isn't about me. It's about Nathan," Taryn deflected in a feeble attempt to change the subject.

"Okay," Tiana conceded to her daughter.

Tiana shook her head with a sigh as she passed the toothpaste to her daughter. Taryn clearly had a thousand things on her mind, and she had every right to, after everything she had been through in less than a year's time. But she knew all too well that if Taryn continued to keep everything locked inside, it would only be a matter of time before she exploded. Taryn was one of the toughest young women Tiana knew, but no one, regardless of how strong they are, is invincible to pain.

As they finished up in the restroom, Taryn quickly applied a touch of makeup on to cover up the dark circles and puffiness under her eyes that, these days, never seemed to go away. Putting her hairbrush and makeup away in her bag, she finished off freshening up with a spritz of perfume before following her mom out of the bathroom.

A comedian as always, they found Noah fake-sleeping on one of the airport massage chairs, instantly snoring obnoxiously as the two women approached him.

"Whoa, it took you guys long enough. Another few minutes, and our plane to go home would have been here already," Noah stated as he stood up stretching and yawning. Everyone let out a slight laugh as they grabbed their things and headed toward baggage claim.

By the time they got there, the belt was already moving in circles as suitcase after suitcase periodically slid down. Noah stood with the carry-ons in the corner as Tiana and Taryn maneuvered through other passengers to get a spot next to the belt. Two years ago, Noah had blown out his back at work and since struggled to lift anything over thirty pounds, so it was up to the ladies to grab their bags.

Sequenced and sparkling, the silver cheer bow seemed to dance atop their suitcase as it slid onto the belt. This was a trick she had learned from her cheer days, traveling with her team for competitions. Using her old bows as markers on the suitcases allowed her and Tiana to spot them easily from across the room. As if the bows waved to her, saying, "Your suitcase is here!"

Two bags behind the first, the next bow shone in the airport light. Noah and Tiana's suitcases were on the belt, slowly making their way around the baggage-claim room toward the two ladies. In one fluid motion, Taryn reached for both suitcases, and seamlessly pulled them from the belt until they were standing upright on the ground. Tiana took them from her and began to roll them toward Noah.

Her eyes searched the belt as Taryn looked for her own suitcase. *There it is*, she thought to herself as she saw the last bow float down the slide toward the belt. This was her favorite bow, tied to some of the happiest memories in her life. The bow they had won championships wearing. The metallic coral blue was a little faded now, but the silver sequin details and sparkling rhinestones still held life in them. Life that Taryn hoped to find again once she figured out how to pick up the pieces of her life and be happy alone.

Grabbing her suitcase off the belt, she maneuvered back through the crowd toward her parents. Together they moved outside of the airport and onto the sidewalk to wait for Nathan.

The San Francisco air welcomed Taryn with a hug that drained all the warmth from her body. Taryn loved the cold weather, but no "Hawaii" jacket was enough to keep her warm right now. Taking a deep breath, she tried to center herself, so she could embrace the day. She refused to let her own issues take away from this special weekend with her family.

"This weekend is for Nathan. You can do this," she whispered the reminder to herself as she closed her eyes and took one more deep breath before catching up with her parents.

"Nathan should be here any minute," Taryn said, looking to her phone as they neared the edge of the sidewalk in the pick-up area.

"You can do this," Taryn repeated to herself on a whisper, smiling as she peered up to see Nathan's car approaching.

2

Nathan

"I'm so excited to see your family again," Sienna said to Nathan as they took the exit toward the airport.

"Same. I'm just worried about Taryn," Nathan said, his voice soaked in worry. "I know it's been nine months now, but if she has that fake-happy act going on that she did during the holidays, I'm going to lose it," he confessed, frustrated.

Thinking back to the holidays, Nathan reflected on how his sister played the perfect hostess, constantly smiling and helping everyone. Throwing herself into entertaining everyone, forcing herself to stay glued together and avoiding questions about what had happened.

"What she went through is rough, Nate. You just let her deal with it in her own way," Sienna replied.

"I know but she's my sister. I can't help but be concerned. Especially when Mom says they hear her cry herself to sleep at night and yet won't talk to anyone about anything when she wakes up. She just goes on pretending she's perfectly fine and throws herself into her work. It's not healthy," Nathan argued.

"Well, at least we have her for a week. Maybe you can get her to open up," Sienna said, trying to ease the tension before they picked everyone up. "*And*...at least she'll be with us all summer too. Maybe a change of scenery will do her some good," she said, remembering their summer plans.

"True, but we'll see. Taryn is six years older than me, so she always pulls her 'I'm the older sister, I worry about you, you don't worry about me' card," Nathan said with a frustrated sigh. "But like you said, she'll be here all summer, so I hope you're right. Hopefully being here will be a good change for her."

When Nathan heard about his sister finalizing her divorce nine months ago he, along with their whole family was, blindsided with absolute shock. Everyone in the family loved Toby, and he had truly become the older brother that Nathan never had. Taryn and Toby were the perfect couple. They balanced each other out, and Toby was the only person who had ever been able to settle Taryn down and seemed to always support his sister regardless of what she was going through in her life. They were together for five years and happily married for another three. They were even talking about starting a family after Taryn finished her doctoral dissertation.

But Toby and Taryn's happily ever after ended before she could even finish her program last December. The strangest thing about the whole situation was that Taryn never told anyone why she filed for divorce or that she had filed for divorce three months before it was finalized and everyone found out. She seemed happy all the time, totally in love, and Toby was even supposed to be on this trip for Nathan's graduation this weekend. The divorce was sudden, out of the blue, and happened so quickly that no one could even process the idea that they were separating before they divorce was finalized.

When anyone asked Taryn what happened, all she would say is "It's better this way" and leave it at that, walking away from the situation or suddenly changing the subject. For being the most out-spoken woman in the family, she wouldn't even defend herself when their cousins began questioning if Taryn did something to push Toby away. She would just shrug her shoulders and say nothing.

Taryn was clearly hiding what really happened during the divorce and was still hiding it nine months later. Why was she hiding the truth? No one knows, but it was something that Nathan desper-ately needed to get to the bottom of to ensure his sister was as "fine" as she claimed to be.

Looking ahead of the other cars flowing into the airport, Nathan kept his eyes on the sidewalk for his dad, Noah. He knew that his dad would stick out like a sore thumb among the other passersby at the airport. In rain, shine, or ninety-degree freezing temperatures, his dad would be in surf shorts and rubber slippers—a true Hawaii boy.

"There they are," Sienna pointed out, about five car paces head of them, smiling as she spotted Nathan's dad first, in shorts and slippers, just as Nathan had predicted.

Nathan brought the car to a stop and parked just a few feet before his family. He never realized how much he appreciated them until he was on his own when he moved to San Francisco for college. But just like they had always been growing up, he could count on them to be there whenever he needed their support.

Getting out of the car, he walked around to his parents and embraced his mom and dad, fighting back happy tears that threatened to fall from his eyes. Pulling back from the hug, he looked down at his mother's glassy eyes.

"Are you crying?" Nathan said with a smirk.

"Shut up. It's just been a while, that's all," replied Tiana with a playful slap on Nathan's shoulder.

"Mom, it's been less than five months since we were home with you guys," Nathan said, letting out a chuckle.

"Again, shut up! It's just been a long four years," Tiana replied with spunk, glaring at her son who was grinning from ear to ear at his mother's rare show of emotion. "I can't believe my baby boy has made it through four years of college, living on the mainland without us! Let me have my moment you, damn kid!" Tiana said as she embraced him in another hug.

"All right all right. Enough mushy stuff. Let's get out of here. I'm hungry," Noah said, trying to rein in his wife. Everyone knew that he was actually the softhearted bag of mush between the two of them, but he had to play it off standing on the side of the road at an airport.

Tiana released her son and began to help Noah push all the bags toward the back of the car. Sienna gave each of them quick hellos and hugs before loading their suitcases into the trunk. Taryn took a deep breath as Nathan approached.

"So proud of you, Nate!" Taryn said as she finally got a turn to hug her younger brother. Even if they were both adults now, she would always see him as her "baby" brother, and Taryn couldn't believe that in twenty-four hours he would officially be a college graduate.

"You doing okay, sis?" Nathan asked her as he pulled away from the hug to grab her suitcases.

"I'm fine," Taryn replied with fake sass. "This weekend is about you! Don't worry about me. I'm good," she persisted, with confidence clearly lacking in her tone.

Nathan eyed his sister suspiciously before shaking his head and walking her suitcase to Sienna.

"She seems okay," Sienna whispered to Nathan as they loaded Taryn's suitcase in the trunk.

"I don't know. I know my sister, and even if it's been a while, that's not her," Nathan replied into her ear as he gave Sienna a hug, grateful for her support, and closed the trunk of the car.

Everyone got into the car and began to settle in for the drive back into the city.

"We're so happy to have you guys here! Nathan's been waiting for this moment since we left Hawaii in January!" Sienna said with a chuckle as she peered over her shoulder to the back seat.

"We've been waiting for this moment since we first dropped him off four years ago," Noah replied, laughing. "It seems like he's been in college forever, eh?" he continued, giving Taryn a little nudge in the arm.

"Yeah," Taryn replied with a sigh, "it's been a while." Taryn turned her gaze back to the window, watching the cars and landscape pass by. It always amazed her that, after passing through stretches of lush, green mountains surrounded by these giant trees and a lake, you're suddenly thrown into a concrete city with buildings on buildings. Seven by seven, she learned when they first moved Nathan up. The city of San Francisco itself was a mere seven miles by seven miles in area, yet immensely compacted with bustling life.

"How 'bout we stop by the apartment so the guys can see you all again? Maybe drop off the suitcases before we head to get food?" Nathan asked as he took the shortcut.

"That's perfect! Then we can stop by Target already and get you guys what you need for the new apartment," Tiana said excitedly.

"Yeah, perfect," Taryn said, looking ahead and seeing Nathan watching her in his mirror. She quickly turned her attention back to the window.

The conversation continued between Tiana, Noah, and Sienna in a blur. Although she was in the car with them, Taryn's mind seemed far away. As he drove, Nathan constantly peered at his sister squished between their parents through the rearview mirror. He could tell just by looking at her that something wasn't okay, and he was determined to figure it out before this trip was over.

3

Taryn

"In just a few weeks, this is no longer gonna be 'home' anymore," Nathan said as he got out of the car and looked up toward the old Victorian-style building. After his first year of living in the dorms at the University of San Francisco, he and three friends found this apartment. No one told them that after the first year of living in the dorms that second-year students were on their own to find a place to stay off campus.

"Hey! Aunty! Uncle! Ti! It's so good to see you guys," Luke said excitedly as he ran down the stairs to hug each of them as Nathan put the car in park.

Luke was one of Nathan's best friends that he made while in San Francisco, and he had even stayed with them on occasion for spring break with Nathan. He was also a key player in supporting Nathan when he was homesick, he was his rave buddy, and he even helped Taryn to pull off Nathan's surprise twenty-first birthday bash in Vegas. He was *hanai* already, an extended part of the family even if he was not blood. He was a brother to Nathan in their books.

"Ti? Are you smoking drugs or something?" Luke asked as he pulled away from their hug. "You're like deteriorating on us, and those dark circles under your eyes are making you look a little scary," he continued, eyeing her and laughing.

"Shut up," Taryn said, laughing and playfully punching Luke in the arm. "I've just been working a lot. Between teaching freshman

English and online classes for USF and finishing my doctoral dissertation, I think I have earned the dark circles under my eyes."

"Okay, well, hopefully you find time for some fun this summer," Luke replied, taking a step back and looking at his best friend's sister. "I know you think you're old and all now, but all that hard work will be for nothing if you don't learn to enjoy life while you're doing it!"

"Right," Taryn scoffed, "says the one who is going to be starting med school in the fall?" Taryn turned to the stairs as Luke grabbed her suitcase from her. "So where's Reggie? And—" Taryn's sentence was cut short with the high-pitched, excited squeals coming down the stairs.

"Aunty! Uncle!" Drew shouted as he bounded down the last few steps and hugged Taryn's parents. "It's been too long!"

Drew was another one of Nathan's roommates and another of his closest friends that he gained while attending USF. Drew and Nathan shared similar bouts of being homesick. Although he wasn't from Hawaii like Nathan was, he was familiar with the tight bonds of family back home on his island of Guam, just south of where Hawaii was in the Pacific.

"Hi, Drew," Taryn said as Drew approached her with arms open wide.

"So you got any new insults to roast me with while you're here, Ti?" Drew replied on a chuckle. Every time he was around, Taryn always had a wise ass remark to make.

"Sadly, no," Taryn replied with a sigh. "It's been a rough one for me. No insults just yet, but don't test me," she added with sass.

"All right," Drew replied as he backed away with his hands up mockingly in the air.

As Drew, Luke, and Nathan began navigating their suitcases up the stairs, Reggie emerged from the doorway at the top of the stairs in his signature khaki shorts and colorful button-up shirt showing just above a much-too-fluffy fleece jacket.

"Hey, guys!" Reggie waved with one hand in his pocket. "How was your flight?"

"Always such a dad, Reg!" Taryn said with a laugh as she reached the top of the stairs and gave Reggie a hug. "We kids have had a long flight, so how 'bout we pull up a chair and talk about it?" she added with a smile and wink.

"Very funny, Ti," Reggie replied with sarcasm laced in his voice. "But you know these three knuckleheads needed someone to play dad, or our apartment would have burned down within the first year!"

"Hey hey hey now, don't spill our secrets dad!" Nathan said, smirking, as he nudged Reggie in the side. "Boys! Dad wants a group hug!" Nathan proceeded to yell.

Suddenly, all the roommates began to jump onto Reggie, hugging him from all angles until he collapsed to the floor. Tiana and Noah just watched in amazement at the friendship that was unfolding right before their eyes. These boys truly made a difference in Nathan's life while he was away at college, and they couldn't be more grateful for their son to have such a wonderful group of friends.

"What are you guys doing?" Emma said as she walked into the foyer, head tilted at the blob of guys piled on each other in the middle of the floor.

"Oh no! It's Mom!" Luke yelled as the boys quickly got up and ran into the other room.

"Thank you," Reggie said with a chuckle as Emma began to dust him off and straighten out his clothes. Emma was Reggie's girlfriend. They had met as freshmen in the dorms, and she was always just one of the guys, a fifth member of their little group. Until Reggie's grandfather passed two years ago. In a moment of comfort, he found his soul mate, and the two of them had been the "parents" of the group ever since.

"Hey, Ti," Emma said as she noticed Taryn still hovering in the foyer.

"Hey, Emma," Taryn replied. "Thanks for helping to look out for my brother and these knuckleheads. Considering what just happened, I doubt they would've made it the last four years without you." She laughed.

"Nooootttt," Reggie dragged as he turned to the two women before scoffing and walking out of the room.

"Thanks, Ti, but we all kinda just took care of each other. Our own little family away from family as we called it," Emma replied. "Are you doing okay, though? Like 100 percent Nathan kinda told us what happened. Just know I'm here if you ever need to have some girl talk, okay?"

"I appreciate that, Emma," Taryn replied with a drawn-out sigh. "But I'm doing okay, as best as I can. Hoping that everyone is right, though. Maybe staying up here this summer for work, getting that change in scenery and just being away from all the reminders of Toby will help," she added as her eyes began to get glassy.

Emma just continued to stare at her, one hand on Taryn's back for support.

"Ugh, enough about me. This trip is for you guys!" Taryn said, wiping away a stray tear that fell from her eyes, taking a deep breath and forcing a smile. "I can't believe four years has gone by that quickly already! Are you ready to graduate?"

"Ready to graduate and be done with homework and studying and crap? Heck yes! Ready for the real world, heck no!" Emma said as both women burst out in laughter. "But I can't stay in college forever, and the nerves about this next chapter in my life makes it kind of exciting."

"Your family flying up from LA for it, right?" Taryn asked.

"Yep! My sister and her husband will be here bright and early tomorrow morning for the day. My parents are flying up this afternoon and will be in town until Wednesday to check in on some of Dad's real estate properties. Thank you, guys, for renting that apartment from him by the way. It's always hard for him to find summer renters, since most of the people who rent that property from him are students who only want to rent it for the school year," Emma said.

"No problem! Thank you for hooking it up and helping us to find somewhere to rent for the summer. If it weren't for you, I would be a homeless summer school teacher, and Nathan would be living out of his office until he found a place of his own," Taryn replied with a laugh.

"Oh and my brother will be up in San Francisco this summer, so if you guys need anything for the apartment or if anything goes wrong, just let him know," Emma said. "I believe he's your age. Twenty-nine, right? And he's single," she added with a smirk.

"That's good for him, Emma," Taryn replied, unsure of what else to say.

"Yeah, he's been here since January filming a movie that just wrapped, and for the past few weeks, he's been helping us out here at the apartment since he has some time. But lucky for you, he'll be here until late August filming a new series for Netflix," Emma continued, her smile growing as she attempted to talk up her brother.

"Well, I'm sure he'll be very busy then. So if anything, I'm pretty handy at DIY stuff, so unless the walls of your dad's place that we're renting starts collapsing on us, I think I can handle it," Taryn replied with a smile. "But even then, I know how to put up beams and drywall," she added in a whisper.

"Okay, Ti. I get it." Emma sighed. "My brother is pretty awesome, though. You'll see. You'll meet him at the graduation tomorrow." On that, she turned and walked out of the room before Taryn could reply.

Oh boy, Taryn thought to herself as her back found the wall, and she slid down to the floor with a sigh. With Nathan trying to find out what happened with the divorce, then having to dodge Emma's attempts to stir the pot with this unknown brother, moving into the new apartment, and the graduation? Taryn felt exhausted already.

"Ti. You ready to get some food and hit Target?" Nathan's voice pulled her from her thoughts. Looking up, her brother's face stared down at her with concern.

"Sure. Let's go," she replied as she peeled herself from the ground and put a smile on her face once more.

*****

The car pulled into the tiny parking lot at Mel's Diner. This was the first place they ate breakfast at when he first arrived in San

Francisco for college, and ever since, it was the first place they ate at every time the family came to visit.

As Taryn got out of the car, she began to stretch her arms toward the San Francisco sky. It always seemed overcast, and even when it was sunny out, the temperatures rarely got higher than seventy degrees even during the summer months—the total opposite weather from Hawaii. But she was looking forward to what she considered as "the cold." For her it meant finding comfort in reading her books, snuggled under a blanket with a cup of steaming hot chocolate to soothe her. She could never do that back home; Hawaii was just too hot.

As the family sat down at a table, they began to ask Sienna what her plans were this summer.

"I'm going to be taking two summer school classes with the University of California, San Francisco, and hopefully that will make it easier to transfer to UCSF in the fall," Sienna began. "Then I'll finish my last two years there, and it'll be closer to home, so it'll be easier to go to class and then go to work and hopefully allow me to contribute more to the rent."

As of last year, Sienna had moved in with Nathan at the apartment and would be living with them as well this summer. After the summer, when Taryn goes back home to Hawaii, Sienna and Nathan would be living on their own together. This would be a huge step not just for Nathan, but also for the family, the thought of him moving in with a girlfriend. But they loved Sienna like their own already and were beyond excited for this next chapter in their life. The summer together with Taryn would be a buffer for this next chapter in everyone's lives.

"Ti, are you excited to teach this summer at USF?" Sienna asked in between bites of her French dip sandwich.

"I don't know why she would teach there. They took so much money from me for tuition, I don't support them at all," Nathan said sarcastically with a mouthful of fries.

"Shut up, Nathan," Taryn replied to her brother. "Yes, I am excited. Teaching online classes for them is one thing, there's no real student-teacher interaction. So to have them offer me a job where I do interact face-to-face with my students is a real honor, and I'm looking forward to it, even if I'm scared beyond my wits," Taryn continued. Turning to Nathan, she added, "But hey. It kind of balances out, right? They take your tuition, and I take money from them for teaching summer school?"

"It only balances if they apply the money that they're paying you toward paying off my student loans," Nathan said with a laugh.

"Okay. I'll be sure to mention that to the Dean of Ed when I start," Taryn replied, laughing sarcastically.

As they finished up their meal, Taryn excused herself to use the restroom. When washing her hands, she threw some water on her face. Damn, the dark circles under her eyes that Luke joked about really did look awful. Patting her face down with a towel, she took a deep breath and applied some brightening powder under her eyes, hoping it would cover the anxiousness and depression weighing on her inside. On her way back to the table, she paid for the till and then headed with her family outside. With their stomachs full, they piled into the car to go to Target to get things for the new apartment.

4

Nathan

Emma's dad, Mr. Bennett, said the apartment would come fully furnished with beds, tables, dressers, couches, etc., but they would need to bring in their own kitchen and cookware as well as toiletries and linens. Taryn, Nathan, and Sienna were so blessed that that was all Mr. Bennett was requesting of them to bring on their own. All other apartments they found that were only leasing for summer required you furnish the entire place yourself. So the fact that Mr. Bennett was providing the place, fully furnished and for such a reasonable price because they were friends with Emma, was a true godsend.

"We're going to go look at the electronics real quick. Meet you guys at the bedding stuff," Nathan said as he began to drag Sienna off before she could stop him.

"Mom and Dad are going to go grab all your folks toiletries, okay? How about you head to the kitchen stuff and start checking out the cookware they have?" Tiana told Taryn.

"Sure," Taryn replied with a sigh as she turned to find the kitchen aisles. As she looked around, she couldn't believe how huge this Target was. Not only did it have two floors, but the layout also seemed much larger, and they offered so many more options for just about everything. Taryn could stay in here for hours and not get bored. Target has always been one of Taryn's favorite stores, and this one was within walking distance from their new apartment and the university she would be working at this summer.

"Nathan, you don't need that game! You already play something similar, if not the same thing already!" Sienna argued as Nathan waited for a Target associate to open the game case.

"You can never have too many games, and the quality of this new edition is supposed to be the best yet," a deep, mysterious male voice responded smoothly from behind them.

As they turned around, Nathan broke out into a smile.

"Hey, Derek! What it do! Emma said you were in the Bay Area now! Every time you've been by the apartment, though, I been at work. It'll be nice to have you around this summer, though!" Nathan said as he shook Derek's hand and went in for a half hug. "See, Sienna, he understands why," Nathan added as he turned back to his girlfriend.

"Ugh. You boys! I give up!" she replied as she walked away toward the bedding section.

"She didn't seem too happy," Derek said with a chuckle, eyes wide. "But yeah, I'm here until August. Shooting a new Netflix series. I'm actually playing a high school senior, so I guess that's a good thing, means I still look young," Derek added as he stroked an invisible beard and turned his head upward to give Nathan a look at his silhouette before breaking out in a laugh.

"That's sick," Nathan replied. "We're just here to grab some stuff for the apartment your dad's letting us rent for the summer." Nathan had only met Derek on the few occasions he came to visit Emma, but he was always cool.

"That's right!" Derek exclaimed. "Wait, if it's just you two, why are you renting the three bedroom? You didn't wanna rent one of dad's smaller apartments?" he asked, confused.

"Oh no. My older sister is going to be staying with us this summer too. She got a professor job to teach summer school courses at USF, and we wanted an extra room just in case my parents come up to visit this summer," Nathan replied.

"Wait. Your sister? I didn't know you had a sister," Derek replied, intrigued.

"Yeah, she's twenty-nine—I think. But she's had a rough year, so I told her this change would be good for her, even if it is just for the summer," Nathan noted.

"Oh, cool. Cool," Derek said. "If I'm not mistaken, it might have been your sister then that Emma was trying to talk up to me."

"Wait, what?" Nathan replied, confused.

"Hey, guys!" Emma interrupted with a smile on her face and a grumpy Sienna attached to her arm.

"Emma, what are you trying to do?" Nathan asked cautiously.

"What? I don't know what you're talking about," Emma replied nonchalantly before looking to Sienna with pleading eyes for approval.

"Don't look at me. This was your idea," Sienna scoffed before shaking her head and looking at the ground.

"Emma?" Derek emphasized his baby sister's name with a sense of sternness.

"Nothing, D! I promise!" Emma replied, standing her ground to the two confused men before her. "It's not a big deal. Nathan's sister is just going to be new to the city, and I thought it would be nice for her to have a friend that's her age. That's all."

The two men eyed her suspiciously.

"Look I'm not saying that Derek isn't a good guy or nothing. It's just that Taryn's been through it this past year, and if she won't even open up to our family, I doubt she'd open up to anyone else. No offense, D," Nathan said with sincerity in his voice.

"None taken," Derek replied to Nathan before turning his attention to his sister. "Even if, I don't know how good of a 'friend' I could be to someone, Emma, if I'm not going to be around. I'm here to film, and I'm not even sure how crazy my call days are going to be. And I don't need my little sister trying to set me up to be 'friends' with anyone," Derek said.

"I get it, guys," Emma said as she put her hands up in the air as an exasperated sign of surrender. "But I'm a female, and as a female I know that sometimes to help us open our hearts again we need a little help from people outside our circle of family and friends," she stated, making circular motions with her hands.

"And I'm sorry to say, D, but you've been throwing yourself into your career so much that you haven't had a 'friend' since your ex-girlfriend six years ago. But I rest my case. We'll just let fate play out itself," she finished confidently before turning to walk away.

"Ugh, that girl. I'm so sorry about her. Sometimes she gets an idea in her head and runs with it, not thinking about the people she's messing with," Derek said, laughing. "I'll see you guys tomorrow, Nathan. Pre-congrats on graduating!" Derek added as he shook Nathan's hand one last time as he turned to follow his sister.

"Yo, Emma is crazy. I can't believe she was going to try set Taryn up with her brother," Nathan said to Sienna as they began to make their way toward the bedding area.

"True, but she does have a point," Sienna replied cautiously as she fell into step beside Nathan.

"What do you mean?" Nathan asked, confused.

"Sometimes it's easier to open up to a stranger who doesn't know your past or anything about you rather than opening up to someone close to you," Sienna stated. "Remember, that's how you and I got close. We met when I was going through it after losing the closest thing I had to a father in my life. Since I didn't know you, it was easier to open up, and look what happened. Not only have you become one of my best friends, but you also helped me to heal and move on."

"I guess. I just know my sister and I don't want her opening up to anyone in any way until she's ready," Nathan said with concern. "She always worried about everyone else, puts everyone else before herself and her own happiness, that I'm afraid one of these days she'll slip so far into her own dark pit that we're going to lose her," he added, looking down with a sigh. He could feel his eyes start to glass over with worry for his sister.

"She'll be okay. We'll make sure she's okay," Sienna encouraged as she wrapped her arms around him from behind, resting her cheek on his back.

Turning down the aisle with different assortments of bedding sets, Nathan spotted his family. Taryn had gone crazy getting cookware and dishes for their kitchen, but Nathan couldn't complain.

Taryn often used cooking as her escape, and it always benefited his stomach and taste buds. It was also clear that his parents had gone over their toiletries checklist twice with an array of items ranging from Clorox wipes to toothpaste piled in the basket as well.

"So you don't want to get any bedding that is white. I know you guys aren't dirty kids, but white does get dirty easier, and you'd have to wash it much more often than normal to keep it from staining," Tiana said to no one in particular as she compared set options and prices.

"I'll take this one," Taryn said as she pulled a nine-piece tan-and-teal bed set from the shelves. "It's about sixty dollars on sale before tax. And, Mom, it's not white," she added sarcastically.

Ignoring her, Tiana lifted the bed set into an empty basket nearby. Noah just leaned on the filled one, laughing to himself as he watched his family with contentment.

"We'll do this, Mom," Nathan said as he slapped a seven-piece black-and-gray bed set, two over from where Taryn pulled hers. "And it's about zero dollars on sale, before tax. And, Mom, it's not white," he added in a high, pitchy voice, mocking his sister.

"Shut up!" Taryn laughed as Nathan slipped the slap she tried to swipe at his shoulder before proceeding to shadowbox with one another like they had always done as kids in the aisle.

The family proceeded to maneuver the two baskets down the aisles, picking out towels and grabbing some snacks before heading to checkout.

Taryn refused to let their parents pay for everything, so she took the responsibility of paying for their bathroom accessories, kitchen-ware, and dishes. Nathan paid for all the food, and her parents paid for the toiletries and bedding before they headed out toward the parking lot.

"Um…this isn't all going to fit in the car," Sienna said with a laugh.

"Nah, we can make it fit," Nathan tried to convince her.

"Nope. She's right, it's not going to fit." Taryn laughed, thinking about how efficient they were getting everything they needed, but not thinking how they would get all this to the apartment.

"Nathan, call Emma and see if her dad has arrived yet, so we can pick up the key to the new apartment and just take all this stuff there already," Sienna said. "In the meantime, I'll call Luke and see if he and Reggie can swing by here and help us transport all this stuff."

Nathan and Sienna began to make their calls as the rest of the family stood there, enjoying the San Francisco day despite their failed plan of transporting their purchases.

"Emma said she and Derek are on their way to pick up their parents from the airport and that they could meet us at the apartment right after," Nathan said.

"Who's Derek? I thought she and Reggie have been and are a thing?" Taryn asked, confused.

"That's just her brother. No big deal," Nathan attempted to reply casually before quickly shooting a glance at Sienna that said, *Don't say anything else.*

"You guys are weird." Taryn laughed, shrugging off the obvious tension between Nathan and Sienna over this Derek person.

Taking a deep breath, Taryn's mind began to wander. Who was this Derek guy, and why did Nathan get all weird when his name was mentioned? Was this the same "brother" Emma was just talking to her about earlier?

Honk honk!

"Did someone call for an Uber transport?" Luke said as he and Reggie pulled up and parked in Reggie's old, SUV behind Sienna's Corolla.

"Yes! Our heroes!" Taryn replied sarcastically as Luke and Reggie got out of the SUV.

"Damn! You guys went in at Target! Two baskets? You must be ballin' as a college professor now, Ti," Luke retorted.

Rolling her eyes, Taryn nudged Luke on the shoulder and began to load things from the baskets into the SUV.

"So where are we taking you guys?" Reggie asked.

"To the new apartment on Sixteenth, the one we're renting from Emma's dad," Nathan replied.

"That's so sick. I wish when we were looking for an apartment at the end of freshman year, Emma's dad had some to rent in SF," Luke complained.

"Well, it wasn't until sophomore year that her dad began to dip into the real estate scene up here," Reggie replied. "After Em's older sister got married and moved away and Derek started traveling for his acting stuff, they wanted to find a way to stay closer to Emma. I guess when you got the money to, it makes sense to buy properties in the city where your baby girl is going to college."

"Damn, if I had that kind of money, I'd buy Hawaii," Luke said sarcastically, making everyone laugh.

Just then, Reggie got a call from Emma, saying they just made it back into the city and were heading to the meet Nathan and his family at the apartment on Sixteenth.

"Okay, we're all packed. I'll meet you there with Nathan, guys," Reggie said over the phone. "Oh no, they needed help fitting everything into the car so Luke and I met them at Target. We'll meet you there, though," he clarified before hanging up the phone.

"Thank you, boys," Tiana said into Reggie's window before getting into the Corolla. "Here we go," she said to her family as the vehicles pulled out of the parking lot and began its short journey toward the new apartment.

5

Taryn

Nathan pulled the car into the driveway of a three-story brownstone on Sixteenth Street in the Richmond District, the intricate cream crown molding on the edges of the building and bay windows giving it character. Waiting at the bottom of the stairs was Mr. and Mrs. Bennett, Emma standing to the side of them. Slowly, everyone started to pile out from the cars. Taryn was completely mesmerized by the beauty of the building.

"Hello! You must be Nathan's family that we've heard so much about!" Mrs. Bennett said as she embraced Tiana in a hug. Standing about five four, Mrs. Bennett wasn't the tallest woman, but she was fierce in her actions. Pulling Taryn out of her awe at the apartment building, Mrs. Bennett enthusiastically continued, "And you must be Taryn! Emma has been talking nonstop about how amazing you are and how you're teaching at the university this summer!"

"Oh. Yes, I'll be teaching two of the summer school courses, Tuesdays and Thursdays. I'm looking forward to the change," Taryn replied with a slight smile.

"I'm Mr. Bennett. Sounds like the university is gaining a wonderful professor this summer," Mr. Bennett responded with a smile as he extended a hand to Noah. "You guys ready to see the apartment?"

"Yes! Thank you so much again for renting it to us for the summer!" Sienna replied excitedly.

"All right then, let's go," Emma said with a big smile plastered on her face as she jingled the keys in the air. Everyone began to follow Emma and her parents up the stairs toward the entrance to the apartment.

"Home sweet home, you guys!" Emma said as she unlocked and pushed the front door open once they reached the third floor of the building. "Well, at least for the summer."

Everyone entered the apartment in complete awe. Despite the dated character of the exterior of the building, this did not foreshadow the beauty of the apartment itself at the slightest. Entering a brightly lit white foyer, you walked into the kitchen with countertops and a large eat-in marble island with light-gray cabinets and stainless-steel appliances to top it off. Stretched before the kitchen were new gray wooden floors that ushered you toward a modern dining table that sat six people comfortably. Just beyond the table was a huge gray sofa nestled in front of a black brick fireplace that was accented with a mounted flat-screen television and built-in bookshelves on either side. Recess lighting throughout the vaulted ceilings of the open-concept living area gave the room the illusion of being much larger than it actually was.

"This apartment is beautiful," Taryn said in awe, trying to take in her new surroundings. "I feel like I've just walked into a page of an HGTV magazine." She giggled.

"Well, we bought this place for a steal when it was being foreclosed and conducted a full renovation on it, kind of like flipping houses on HGTV," Mrs. Bennett explained.

"But instead of selling, we wanted to use it as a rental property investment. When Emma was in college, we saw how much she and her friends would struggle to find a decent apartment at a fair price to rent in the city. So we figured it would pay off in the long run because, based on the apartment and the price we'd rent it for, we'd always have a clientele of renters interested," Mr. Bennett finished.

"The two main rooms have their own en suite restrooms and walk-in closets," Mrs. Bennett added proudly. "And the guest bedroom has a full bath just off to the side."

"Well, if you don't have anyone to rent after the summer's up, for the school year that is, we might be interested in just extended our lease with you guys beyond summer if we can't find another place," Nathan noted. "It's better we rent from people we know and trust than try and put our faith in complete strangers, right?"

Everyone laughed, but the apartment was no joke. For the size and location, the rental price was a dream!

"Okay. Well, now that you guys have seen the living space, we'll leave you to explore and pick out your rooms," Mrs. Bennett said with a smile. "And if you need anything this summer, please feel free to call our son Derek. His apartment is a block over, and he'll be here until August if you need anything for the apartment. We've left his number on the fridge."

"Yes, don't hesitate to call him," Mr. Bennett added. "Speaking of, we have to go pick him up from that meeting with his castmates for this new show he's filming. It was a last-minute thing to go over call times or something? But who knows." Mr. Bennett chuckled at his own joke. He never understood the passion his son had for acting as he and both his daughters were into business. But it did make his boy happy, and that was all he could have hoped for.

"Well, we'll see you guys tomorrow at the graduation! Have a good evening!" Mrs. Bennett said with a smile before turning and heading out the door with her husband.

"I'll meet you guys back at the boys' apartment to help pack and clean up after I have dinner with my parents this evening," she said to Reggie with a kiss on his cheek before following behind her parents. "Remember, don't hesitate to call Derek. Okay, Ti?" Emma threw over her shoulder with a wink as she hurried down the stairs.

"Reggie, your girl is too much sometimes," Luke said, laughing and elbowing him in his side. "Come on, we gotta beat them to the apartment before she shows up with her parents and they see the pigsty of a mess you two have been living in."

"Really? It's not that bad, Luke. We just haven't had time to clean up, with finals and everything," Reggie argued.

"Riiigggghhhttt," Luke dragged. "Come on. We'll be back later, guys!" With a wave, he and Reggie headed down the stairs.

In the new apartment alone, the family took in their surroundings with a long sigh before looking at each other.

"Wow. My two babies are going to be living here this summer," Tiana said, eyes glazing over with tears threatening to flow down her cheeks. "My babies aren't babies anymore."

"Stop, Tiana," Noah urged as he pulled his wife in for a hug. "Come on, let's go check out the kids' rooms before they make it all messy with their endless crap." He laughed as he dragged her into a room just off the kitchen.

"Ti, how 'bout you go pick your room first, since you are the oldest and you're paying for the rent? Sienna and I will head back to the boys' apartment and bring over all your suitcases," Nathan said as he and Sienna headed toward the door.

"Sounds like a plan," Taryn replied with a sigh as she found herself drawn to the massive collection of books on the shelves lining the fireplace.

"All right, we'll be back," Nathan replied as they left.

Being that she taught English, Taryn always had a love for books. Escaping into a good novel was the perfect distraction for her when she had down time during the divorce. Her novels transported her to a world where her problems didn't exist, and that drew her closer and closer to her passion for reading. Running her fingers across the spines of the books near the fireplace, head tilted to the side to read the titles, she was completely in awe of the Bennett book collection. She knew exactly what she would be doing this summer when she wasn't teaching—she'd be burying her nose in this collection.

I gotta find a good bookstore nearby, Taryn thought to herself. *A good book and a nice cup of coffee at a café*, her thoughts began to wander. Something so simple sounded just perfect to help her find peace in her life again.

"You know, escaping into the stories in books aren't going to help you move on with your life," Tiana said, hands on her hips as she emerged from the bedroom staring at her daughter.

"Huh?" Taryn replied, confused.

"Honey, in order to move on you need to face what happened. Not run away to a storybook so you don't have to deal with it," Tiana retorted.

"I am dealing with it, Mom. Just in my own way," Taryn replied defensively.

"Hey, Ti, you're going to want to claim dibs on this master suite," Noah interrupted, eyes wide and smiling as he emerged from the room behind Tiana.

"It doesn't matter, right?" Taryn said, a tad annoyed at the comment her mom just made.

"When you see this room it will matter," Noah argued with a laugh. "You have your own little balcony that overlooks the city, and it's already equipped with an outdoor heater, so you can stay warm when you read on the chair they got out there," he said slyly.

"Seriously?" Taryn said in disbelief. Her dad often exaggerated his descriptions so she wasn't sure if he was truly excited for this room, or if he was just trying to make her excited for this next chapter in her life.

As Taryn entered the room, she froze and her mouth fell open. Eyes wide, she scanned the room inch by inch, completely amazed by what was before her. The room was absolutely breathtaking. The gray floors from the living space continued into the room but was brought to life with clean, sleek furniture and details filling everywhere she could see. Off to the right when you entered the room was a cream, two-seater sofa with black decorative pillows. Just beyond that in the corner of the room, framed with a beautiful window overlooking the street, was a black-stained wooden desk with a stainless-steel frame and built in shelves off to one side.

Moving her gaze across the room was a huge, king-size bed lavished in a fancy gray polyester pin tuck duvet with more pillows than she would ever need. As she walked toward the bed, a huge walk-in closet accented with gray built-in organizers, drawers, and a dresser came into view. Next to it was the door to her en suite bathroom. Entering the bathroom, clean white marble flooring came into view with the same gray cabinets and marble countertops accenting his-and-her sinks with a small vanity area in between. A secondary door led to a toilet in its own private room, accented with a huge rain shower and bench on one side and a jet-soaking tub on the other.

As you exited the bathroom, a quaint balcony came into view on the opposite side of the bed. Just as her dad described, a cozy, two-seater patio chair sat on the balcony with a small side table to one side and an outdoor heater to the other side. Entering back into the room and taking a seat on the foot of the bed, Taryn tried to take it all in.

"Wow." She sighed. "They really outdid themselves with this room!" Taryn continued to look around her new room for summer in awe.

"What does this button do?" her dad said as he pushed a small circular button next to her light switches. He was like a little kid playing with a new toy.

A flat-screen television slowly swung down, emerging from the ceiling before positioning itself just above the couch and directly across the foot of the bed.

"Whoa! That's so cool!" Noah exclaimed as he went to hit the same button again.

"Dad! Stop!" Taryn laughed. "You're going to end up breaking it!" Getting up from the bed, she began to usher her dad out of the room.

"So I guess you're choosing that room?" Tiana asked curiously.

"I think so. Let's go check out the other room to make sure it's enough space for Nathan and Sienna," Taryn replied as she made her way through the living space and down a small corridor toward another room. "I wouldn't want to pick the bigger room if they don't have enough space in theirs. I mean, it's just me. They have two of them to fit in a room."

Turning the doorknob on the other room, the same reaction they've been having all day to the apartment took hold of the three family members.

"This room is bigger than our master bedroom back home," Noah said as they entered the space.

Similar to the first room they checked out, the same gray wood floors welcomed you in. Right when you entered, there was a gray two-seater sofa, this time accented with white decorative pillows instead of black ones. Just beyond that in a corner next to the bed was a duplicate desk of the one from the first room. A queen-size bed took center stage in the room accented on either side with a little nightstand. A few feet from the foot of the bed, against the opposite wall, was a gray dresser with its own flat-screen television above it. To the right of the television was a large walk-in closet with similar organizers and drawers. To the left, the door to an en suite bathroom. The bathroom was themed the same as all else in the house, marble flooring and countertops with gray cabinets. A white toilet sat in the far corner of the room, next to the his-and-her sinks, across from a rain shower. A smaller soaking tub sat next to the shower.

"Wow. This room is spectacular and spacious too despite not having a small balcony," Taryn observed.

"Well, honey, I think this is more than enough space for Nathan and Sienna," Tiana stated. "You take the room with the balcony, so you can get some fresh air if you need to, and you'll have a nice place to escape into a book on occasion," she continued as she sat at the edge of the bed, smiling up at her daughter.

"Yeah, he'll be fine in here, and quite frankly I think it's safer for the two of them to not have a balcony," Noah added.

Tiana and Taryn looked at him in confusion.

"Well, when they're drunk, you won't have to worry about them going on a balcony and falling over, duh," he responded with a laugh.

"That is not funny, Noah," Tiana argued with a chuckle as she playfully hit her husband on the shoulder. "All right, now that you know your rooms, help us go get settled in the guest room. I think I just heard Nathan and Sienna come back."

"Yes, ma'am," Noah stated as he saluted his wife.

Rolling her eyes, Tiana walked out of the room. Noah and Tiana following suit behind her to find that Nathan and Sienna had already miraculously brought all the suitcases up to the third floor themselves.

"Time to unpack!" Sienna said excitedly.

"Did you pick your room, Ti?" Nathan asked.

"Yeah, I'll take the one off the kitchen," Taryn replied. "Both got a lot of room and beautiful bathrooms, but I kinda want the one with the balcony, so I can sit out there and read. Is that okay?"

"That's perfect!" Sienna replied. "I'm afraid of balconies. I watched too much *Special Victims Unit* episodes, and I'd be too scared to sleep with a balcony next to my bed." Sienna shuddered to herself before taking a bag of her things into their room.

"Yeah, like that didn't just make me worry that now you're going to have a balcony giving perverts access to your room with you in it all alone," Nathan said sarcastically, shaking his head to Taryn.

"You guys are so crazy. It's fine," Taryn said. "I've watched enough of those shows too to make sure that I won't become anyone's 'victim' even with a balcony next to my bed." Taryn laughed.

Slowly, everyone began to move their suitcases into their designated rooms. Tiana and Noah unpacked in the guest room completely, even if they were only going to be staying for the week. Taryn slowly moved her belongings into the walk-in closet as Nathan started to hook up all his electronics in their room. After unpacking her suitcases, Taryn moved into the kitchen to put away all the dining and kitchenware that they bought from Target as Tiana began to put away and organize all the toiletries. Time seemed to move in slow motion as Taryn continued to take in her new surroundings.

Later that evening, after they put away everything they purchased, even putting the extra bedding they bought into the linen closet in the laundry room and unpacking what they could in their new rooms, they sat down for dinner.

"I'm going to get so fat this summer if everywhere to eat around here does delivery like this," Taryn said as she took another bite of her chicken alfredo.

"Yep. A majority of restaurants in the Bay Area do the food-delivery services, so most times you don't even need to leave the house to get a good meal," Sienna explained.

"And they do late-night delivery too. Some places stay open until 2:00 a.m. sometimes," Nathan added excitedly. "We know because we're guilty of making those late-night orders when we got home from the club."

As the conversation continued and filled the apartment as everyone helped to tidy up after dinner, Taryn couldn't help but sit back and smile with contentment. Even if it had been a rough year, one thing she would forever be grateful for was the people in front of her. Unlike most of her students she taught back in Hawaii, she was lucky enough to have a tight-knit family who she could always rely on to be there for her through everything. No matter where they would go in life or what this next chapter held for them, she knew she would always have these wonderful people to support her. She just didn't know how supportive they would be when they found out the secrets behind her divorce.

"Good night, everyone. See you bright and early," Tiana and Noah said as they hugged their kids and disappeared into the guest room.

"Good night, Ti," Sienna said as she too turned to head into her and Nathan's room.

"Good night," Taryn replied as she finished wiping the last few dishes to put away.

"Ti, you good?" Nathan asked before calling it a night.

"I'm good," she replied with a sigh.

"You're going to talk to me eventually about it, Ti," Nathan said on a frustrated sigh. "You can't keep this up all summer with me. I know you well enough to know you're not good."

"Nathan," Taryn said with a serious tone. "This weekend is about you, okay? And if it eases your mind, I promise you'll be the first I come to when I'm ready to talk about everything, okay?"

"Okay." Nathan sighed and walked away, feeling defeated.

After putting the last clean dish in the cabinet, Taryn headed into her room. As she sat on the balcony to get some fresh air, her brother's words resonated in her mind. He was right. She wasn't doing good, but she felt she had no choice but to hold it together. Not just for her family, since they were still in the dark about why she and Toby got a divorce, but also because she didn't want to let Toby win. Call it stupidity or competitiveness, but seeing how well his life was going now that she wasn't in it was killing her more than the divorce did itself. She knew she couldn't keep this act up for much longer.

6

Derek

"You look beautiful, Em," Derek said as he hugged his sister one last time as they dropped her off for the commencement ceremony. "My little sis is all grown up," he continued with a fake cry.

"Geez. I know you're an actor and all, but you don't need to 'act' around us. Just be normal for once," Emma said as she smacked her brother in his shoulder.

Staring at each other hard for a few moments, you could feel the tension between Derek and Emma build before the two suddenly broke out into hysterical laughter.

"You guys are weird," Janie said, laughing at her two younger siblings as she stood watching next to her husband. Even if they were six years apart, Derek and Emma had always seemed to have a special connection. They were each other's partner in crime growing up with Janie on the sidelines as a second motherly figure to them.

"Hey, Bennetts," Reggie said as he approached the family through the crowd of graduates saying their farewells to their families.

"Hey, Reg!" Emma said as she jumped up and wrapped herself in a hug around him.

"Hey! Hey! Hey! Hands off my boyfriend," Derek said jokingly as he pulled Reggie's arm and gave him a side hug.

"Hey, D," Reggie said with a laugh.

Reggie was the first and only boyfriend of Emma's that Derek ever liked and got along with. He came from a good family, had good morals, and truly seemed to care for his sister based solely on who she was as a person. It also helped that Derek had been in San Francisco filming a movie since January, so he really got to know Reggie over the last few months. Derek could also appreciate that Reggie surrounded himself with an amazing group of friends who were loyal, down to earth, and all-around good people so he never had to worry about Emma being around any negative energy in college. Reggie's roommates had also been friends with Emma since their freshman year at the University of San Francisco too, and they had all taken care of and protected his sister when he wasn't there these last few years.

"You ready to graduate, bro?" Derek asked him.

"Oh yeah!" Reggie exclaimed. "I'm beyond over all these finals and papers. I'm ready to get to work."

"Good to hear, my boy," Mr. Bennett said.

"Come on, Reg, I think I heard the chancellor. We better head inside," Emma said, dragging Reggie away from her family. "See you guys on the other side!" she added as she waved goodbye to them.

Inside the huge chapel, people were squished together in the pews, all trying to push forward to get a good view of the stage where the graduates would be crossing over into the real world. Sitting at the edge of the right side of the bench, Derek was thankful he chose to do a dressy-casual style for this occasion with blue jeans, a button-up dress shirt with an unbuttoned polyester suit jacket, and his black Converse shoes. It would have been way too hot with all these people in here to sit comfortably in a full-dress suit.

"Hey, Mr. and Mrs. Bennett," a sweet voice drifted into his ears above all the chatter filling the chapel.

"Hey, Taryn! We're so excited! We'll see you outside when it's done," his mother replied.

As he turned to look toward his mother, he caught a glimpse of the back of a young woman dressed in matte black, flowing slacks, and an emerald-green silk sleeveless top with a bow tied in the center of her back. Long dark brown waves cascaded over one shoulder as she walked with confidence toward another pew, just a few feet in front of them. She sat at the end of the pew next to a man, a woman, and a familiar face. Sienna's face, Nathan's girlfriend. His sister's roommate's girlfriend.

"Hey, who are those people sitting with Nathan's girlfriend?" Derek whispered beyond Janie and her husband to his mother.

"Um, Reggie and Luke's families," Mrs. Bennett replied, confused. "You met them before, why are you asking?"

"Duh, dummy. Who else would be sitting with her? Those roommates are so close that their families are family to each other already," Janie said sarcastically.

"Ugh," he said, brushing off his sister's response. "No, I mean the people on the other side of Sienna, to the left side of the pew. With the girl that said hi to you guys?" he tried to clarify.

"That's Nathan's family," replied Mrs. Bennett, slightly exasperated. "The people sitting in front of us a few pews forward, next to Sienna, is Nathan's family. The people on the other side of her to the right is the Reggie and Luke's families. And in front of Nathan's family on the left is Drew's family. Now be quiet! The ceremony is starting soon!"

As the ceremony commenced, Derek couldn't help but feel drawn toward this mysterious girl in green sitting with whom he assumed to be Nathan's parents. He met Nathan before and loved him. Derek was impressed with his commitment to family, friends, loyalty, and respect for everyone. Because of the neighborhood Nathan grew up in, he never hesitated to stand up for his friends, and Derek could always trust that whenever they went out, Nathan would protect them if worse came to worse. Nathan was also a very logical thinker and was the one person who could reason with Emma without question. Even Reggie would go to Nathan to pick apart their arguments and make Emma think reasonably. Although he knew Nathan had an older sister back in Hawaii, he didn't know much else about Nathan's family.

Slowly, the processional continued as names of the graduates were called one by one, families cheering throughout the chapel as their loved one made their way across the stage to receive their degrees.

"Emma…Bennett," the chancellor called.

"Whoo! Go, Em!" Janie cheered.

"Yeah, Em! Whoo!" Derek echoed.

Looking over toward their parents, Derek smiled as he saw happy tears form in his mother's eyes as she watched the baby of the family reach such a huge accomplishment in her life. More names were called, and Derek's attention turned back toward Nathan's family. Searching the row of people in front of him, he noticed that the girl in green had disappeared. *Oh no*, he thought as he looked down for Nathan's name in the program and realized that they were getting closer to calling him up for his degree. She's going to miss it. Looking around the chapel frantically for this stranger, his attention was yanked back to the stage when he heard Nathan's name being called.

"Nathan...Okata," the chancellor's voice rang out.

Suddenly the chapel was filled with one loud and powerful cheer. It was not a common cheer you'd hear at graduations in California, and it sounded as if it were almost part of a tribal chant. Derek was stunned as he stood and leaned forward in his chair toward where the sound came from.

"Chee-hoo! Cheu! Cheu! Cheu!"

The mysterious yell continued to fill the chapel as Nathan received his degree from one of the deans in the center of the stage. As Derek scanned the front of the room, he caught a glimpse of emerald huddled down near the front of the stage where he heard the yelling come from, a cell phone camera recording held up to capture Nathan's moment.

Wait, that can't be, Derek thought to himself as a small smile spread across his face, wondering if that huge voice that came from the front was Nathan's sister who was no longer sitting in the pew next to his parents. It couldn't be Nathan's parents because they were still sitting next to Sienna.

Standing up and turning to the back of the chapel, her face finally came into his vision like a blinding light, and he was no longer captivated by the yelling voice he was searching for, but it was her beauty that now had his full attention. She glided gracefully down the aisle toward the back of the chapel, each step seemingly floating as her hair bounced from side to side. Her dark-brown eyes seemed to smile with pride as she walked toward her parents, a glow of beauty following her. Fluidly, she knelt down next to the pew, picking up a few full bags before standing again and flipping her hair back over her shoulders. The most gorgeous smile filled her face, outlined by luscious pink lips. Crinkling her nose and tipping her head toward the back exit, Sienna stood up and made her way into the aisle.

The two women began to walk toward the back exit of the church together. Slowly but surely it seemed as if they were approaching Derek and his family.

"Pull it together, D! You're drooling," Janie whispered to her brother as her eyes went back and forth between Derek and Nathan's sister. Janie giggled to herself. She'd never seen her brother so smitten over someone like this before.

"Shut up," Derek replied, trying to snap himself out of his state of awe, but his eyes remained on Nathan's sister.

Sienna and Nathan's sister approached their pew.

"We're going to go save a spot in the courtyard for the boys to meet and set up their signs already," Sienna whispered to Mrs. Bennett. "Taryn couldn't sleep last night, so she made them signs to take a picture with."

Taryn, Derek thought to himself. That was her name. It was a beautiful name for a breathtaking girl. Despite Janie's reminder that he was making it beyond obvious that he was captivated by her, he couldn't help but continue to stare.

"Taryn, that was so sweet of you," Mrs. Bennett replied.

"It was nothing. I enjoy my late-night Target runs, and I was still on Hawaii time anyways," Taryn said with a giggle as that same radiant smile emerged again.

"Well, see you girls outside," Mrs. Bennett said as the two girls nodded and turned on their heels toward the exit.

Taryn, Derek thought to himself again as he made a feeble attempt to refocus on the awards ceremony. Slowly, one by one, the names of Nathan's other roommates—the boys Emma have deemed as her "other brothers"—were called, but the only name on Derek's mind was Taryn.

Surprisingly, the sun was shining outside without a cloud in sight for the first time in weeks. It made the green of the grass in the courtyard seem even more so lush and alive. His family made their way toward the opposite end of the courtyard. Reggie's, Nathan's, and their other roommates' families were already there. The chancellor had dismissed all families from the chapel prior to releasing the graduates, so there was less of a crowd of people trying to exit all at once.

Medium white three-by-five cardboard poster boards were lined up next to one another, each with one of the boys' names written with glitter in green and outlined in gold. From left to right the signs read "Luke, Nathan, Reggie, and Drew." In the center another poster board had Emma's name on it in gold glitter but with green outline.

She did this all in one night? Derek thought to himself as they approached the other families, each assuming a place behind the sign for their graduate that Taryn had made. His eyes scanned each sign in amazement.

"Taryn dear, you really outdid yourself! Thank you so much for including one for our Emma," Mrs. Bennett said as she pulled Taryn into a hug.

"It was nothing, Mrs. Bennett. Emma was one of the boys, like a sister to them, so of course I had to make her one too!" Taryn exclaimed excitedly. "Quite honestly, it occupied me last night," she added with an awkward laugh. "I've been having trouble sleeping lately, so at least I had something to do." A full, ear-to-ear smile brimmed from her full lips as cute dimples emerged on each cheek, and her eyes squinted at the outer corners.

Standing there awkwardly with his hands in his pockets, Derek couldn't help but stare at Taryn. Watching as the sun kissed her face and made her glow with a radiance he had never seen before. Even with makeup, there was a natural beauty about her that had him in complete awe.

"Chee-hoo!" Taryn suddenly yelled, cupping her hands around her mouth and tilting her head back, using her diaphragm to push the cheer across the courtyard.

It was the same tribal-sounding yell that he had heard in the chapel during the graduation ceremony, and it snapped Derek out of his awkward state. A smile spread across his face as he saw the excitement on Taryn's as her voice continued to ring across the grass toward the graduates.

That was her, he thought to himself with a chuckle. *How does such a huge voice come out of that tiny body?* he thought, absolutely amazed. Taryn showed no shame in celebrating her brother graduating and smiled proudly as she continued to *chee-hoo* while other people began to stare in their direction.

The group of their graduates slowly made their way across the university lawn, Nathan leading the way, following his sister's voice.

When he came into plain view, Nathan stopped, cupped his hands to his mouth, and returned his sister's cheer.

"Chee-hoo!" he yelled to the sky, bending down on one knee.

"Cheeu-cheeu-cheeu!" Taryn replied to him.

It was truly a sight to see, and Derek's amazement at Taryn was growing by the minute.

The five gradates stood by their signs for what seemed like an endless number of pictures. Pictures with each other, with family, and with other friends that came to congratulate them. Their leis piling on their shoulders up to their eyes. At the end of it all, the five of them popped and shook champagne bottles toward the sky, being careful not to wet anyone nearby. The entire time, Taryn stared with pride at her brother, capturing each aspect of this moment with her camera. Derek was staring at Taryn with utter intrigue. Everyone circled around one another.

"All right!" Nathan stated, rallying their group together. "Lunch with the families and then meet back at the apartment for the send-off?" he asked as he looked to his roommates and Emma for confirmation on their plans.

"Yessir!" Luke replied.

"Sounds like perfection," stated Drew.

"We're in," stated Reggie as Emma nodded her approval.

"Parents invited too?" Nathan's dad asked jokingly.

"Sorry, Uncle. No parents allowed tonight," Emma said as she comfortingly patted him on his shoulder. "But older siblings should come, right? Party with us before we are in the 'real world' with them? Just once?" Emma asked sneakily as she gave Sienna a sly smile and wink.

"I don't know, Em," Derek said, sure he would end up babysitting his little sister if he went to the boys' apartment for a send-off party.

"Come on, D! Please! One time. I've rarely got to drink or hang out with you since I turned twenty-one because you're always traveling to film! Please!" Emma pleaded with big puppy-pout eyes to her brother.

Taryn, just hung back quietly watching the exchange.

"All right," Derek said, sighing heavily. "But I'm not babysitting you," he added jokingly.

"Promise!" Emma exclaimed, happy with her small victory. "Ti, that means you have to come by too!" she added, turning everyone's attention to Taryn.

Frozen like a deer in headlights, Taryn's self-assured persona suddenly changed. Her eyes seemed unsure, and Derek noticed that she began to fidget under the pressure. *I wonder why she's so hesitant?* Derek thought to himself. Continuing to watch her, for the first time their eyes met from across the group of friends. Her dark-brown eyes seemed to pierce right into his soul, and he suddenly felt drawn to her, like she had hooked into him physically somehow in that moment. It was as if she felt the same thing, and suddenly she broke their eye connection and looked to the ground.

"Five bucks says Emma won't get Ti to come by," Nathan whispered to Sienna, knowing the stubbornness of his sister.

"Five bucks and a large coffee says Emma can," Sienna whispered back. "I've never known Emma to settle for someone telling her no."

"You know, I'm going to wake up really early tomorrow to go over there to help you guys clean, fix stuff, and pack. So maybe it's not the best idea for me to come out tonight," Taryn said, shaking her head, trying to find an excuse not to go.

"That's perfect! You can just sleep over tonight at the apartment with us, so you don't have to wake up so early tomorrow!" Emma plotted.

Minutes passed with Emma giving an intense stare toward Taryn. Derek was closely watching and waiting to see how Taryn was going to respond to his sister, the master arguer of their family. Everyone laughed as Taryn let out a slight chuckle and clenched her eyes shut, dropping her head before sighing heavily.

"But if we're up all night I won't have the energy to help you guys out as I would be able to if I didn't go out. I'll just see you guys tomorrow. It's your night, you guys celebrate," Taryn finally replied as she lifted a slight gaze and squinted eyes toward Emma. She was seemingly preparing herself for Emma's comeback.

And boy did Emma have one.

"Well," she started. "You're right. It is our night, and since it's our night, we should get to celebrate how we want to celebrate. And we want to celebrate with our older siblings. Hence, you need to come because if not, you'd be ruining how we want to celebrate our graduation. And if cleaning is going to be that big of a thing for you tomorrow, you can start with making sure we don't make that big of a mess tonight." A huge smile spread across Emma's face as she tilted her head with utter sass.

"Em!" Derek scolded his sister. "You can't peer pressure a person into doing what you want by making them feel bad."

The jaws of all the boys and Sienna dropped with big eyes turning toward Taryn, waiting for her reaction.

"Fine," she said with utter defeat in her voice, slowly raising her eyes toward Derek. "Thanks for trying but she's right," she said to him with a gorgeous smile that almost knocked him on his behind. Turning her attention to Emma, she added, finding her confidence again: "I'll come but you need to compromise with me and let me do some cleaning tonight before I drink with you folks. Okay? Deal?"

"Deal!" Emma replied with a smile. Running across the group, Emma pulled Taryn in for a hug.

As Taryn embraced Emma back, a smile spread across her face as she suddenly caught the gaze of Derek once again. As their eyes locked, Derek mouthed a thank-you at Taryn as she nodded back.

"Drooling," Janie whispered behind Derek.

"Shut up!" Derek replied with a smile.

He couldn't help himself, though. Now that Taryn was going tonight, he had something to look forward to.

7

Taryn

After lunch at a dim sum restaurant, Taryn, Nathan, Sienna, Tiana, and Noah made their way back to the summer apartment. Tiana organized the leis on the dining room table with Sienna as Nathan went to take a shower. Noah lounged on the sofa, clicking through the channels, and Taryn went to pack a night bag to take with her to the boys' apartment that night.

I can't believe I'm going to a college party, Taryn thought to herself, already exasperated by the thought. She packed a night bag with everything she would need to clean the house the next day, from extra clothes to some go-to cleaning supplies. Jumping in the shower, she removed her makeup and let the warmth of the water take control of her as she closed her eyes in relaxation. As she shampooed her hair, her thoughts began to drift, pulling her back to that dark moment as she froze despite the heat of the shower filling the spaces around her.

"Ti, I'm sorry. I didn't mean for any of this to happen!" Toby's voice echoed in her thoughts. Shocked from the news, she froze as every inch of her heart and lungs seem to constrict to the point where she could physically feel the air and blood drain from her body. "I love you. I do, but this just isn't working anymore. I can't give you what you want, and I refuse to be the person to stand in the way of your happiness." Her voice carried the words from her mouth, her brain, and her heart—no longer in control. No matter how much she wanted their marriage to work, no matter what she would do to try and fix it, things would never be the same. "Ti, don't do…do this, please. I'll fix this. We can figure this out together. Please! I need you." The memory of Toby's pleads still pierced every inch of her soul. Whoever said words don't hurt you was truly mistaken. Every word, every inflection, created internal, invisible cuts on her heart that Taryn was unsure if she could ever heal from. Forcing herself to be strong. "No. We're done, Toby. I'm sorry. I just can't do this anymore."

As the thought of her walking away in that moment played back over and over in her head, tears began to burn her cheeks as she whispered to herself over and over again, "I'm sorry."

A knock on her bathroom door pulled her back to reality. She quickly choked back the river of tears that began threatening to stream from her eyes.

"Yes?" she said in a deep breath, trying to steady her voice.

"We're leaving in fifteen minutes. You almost ready?" Nathan's voice rang through the door.

"I'll be out in five," Taryn replied.

Quickly lathering her hair in conditioner and washing her body, Taryn rushed to finish her shower, unsure of how long she had been in here. Taking the towel off the rack, she stepped out of the shower, the tile cold under her feet. She quickly wiped off and wrapped her hair in the towel as she applied a little powder to brighten up under her eyes. Taryn threw on her lacy underwear, black cheer shorts, a white tank top, and a zip-up black athletic jacket. Drying her hair a little bit more, she ran her brush though the tangles before putting it up into a bun with her favorite clip.

As she exited the bathroom, she checked her night bag to make sure she had everything she would need for tomorrow: her shorts, a sports bra, a tank top, an extra shirt, and her toothbrush. She quickly grabbed her phone and charger, shoving them into the bag and her wallet as she exited her room.

"You ready?" Nathan asked. "You were in the shower a long time."

"Yeah, sorry. The hot water just felt so good, I kinda lost track of time," Taryn said suspiciously. "Let's go," she quickly added with a smile as she noticed everyone in her family was just staring at her with concern in their eyes.

"You want to get some coffee first, Ti?" Sienna suggested, breaking the tension.

"That would be amazing," Taryn replied, hugging Sienna, silently thanking her for her support and help to get away from the awkwardness that was slowly filling the room.

"Okay," Nathan said, sighing, as he got up shaking his head.

"Have fun tonight and be safe, you guys," Tiana said in a motherly voice.

"We will," Sienna replied. "Good night."

"We'll be there around 10 a.m. tomorrow morning," Noah added, walking them to the door.

"Good night, guys! See you tomorrow!" Taryn replied as she hurried down the stairs with her bag, with Sienna following behind her.

"Watch your sister, Nathan. She's acting all weird again," Tiana reminded him.

"I will. Lock the doors. Love you, guys!" Nathan replied as he hugged his parents before following Sienna and Taryn to the car.

"Whoo! Let's get this party started!" Luke exclaimed excitedly when they got to the boys' apartment. In the living room, Luke and Drew already set up the beer pong table and a poker area. The windowsill and the top of their fireplace was lined with different types of alcohol, ranging from beers to soju to vodka. On the television mounted on the wall, an electronic dance music (EDM) station was playing.

"This is going to be a long night." Taryn sighed quietly to herself as she took in the scene before her. "How many people are you expecting to come tonight?" she asked Luke.

"Us, our girlfriends, a few of our friends from UCSF, and the 'older siblings' as Emma argued." Luke laughed. "That's why you're here, right?"

"Oh shut up," Taryn argued sarcastically. "I'm just here to get a head start on cleaning, and being invited by Emma was just the perfect excuse. I'll just watch you guys get wasted," she added with a laugh.

"Don't count on it," Drew said, coming up behind her and patting her on the shoulder. "You gotta have a few drinks with us," he said as if she had no choice.

As the night progressed, it was surprisingly chill for the amount of alcohol the boys had bought. They had a total of about twenty of their closest friends show up. Once the party started to gain life, Taryn used the opportunity to slip away and look around the apartment to assess exactly how much cleaning and repairs they would need to do the next day to prep the boys to move out.

Leaving her flats on, she was relieved as they slowly began to stick to the floor as she walked down the hallway, taking a right into their kitchen. A pungent smell invaded her nose, making her tilt her head, eyes clenched, as she tried to center her breath despite the sourness in the air. Slowly looking around, she saw that there were a handful of dirty dishes in the sink yet to be cleaned, and a peek into the fridge showed a mountain of leftover containers from various restaurants that looked to be over a week old. Opening the cupboards and checking the nonperishables, she found food that was expired for two years already.

Making a mental checklist in her mind, she was already mapping out what needed to be thrown away, and it seemed as if she would need a ton of trash bags. Finding their bottle of Dawn soap and a spray bottle of Clorox under the sink, she poured some soap and sprayed some Clorox onto the dishes in the sink to soak overnight.

Heading down the hallway, she made her way into the one bathroom all four boys shared. Taking a deep breath before entering, Taryn tried to mentally prepare herself for what she would find. Opening the door, she thought her eyes would bulge from her head as her mouth inadvertently dropped in utter shock.

Right off the back, you could see mold making its way up the corners of the wall to the ceiling and lining the base of the shower as a result of the lack of ventilation the restroom had. The shower itself was stained with soap scum and calcium buildup. Orange-brown gunk that Taryn didn't even recognize lined their sink. Long hair, assumingly from the girls, gathered in different corners on the floor. In the entire bathroom, she was surprised the toilet was the cleanest as she lifted the seat to only see some pee droppings dried up.

"How could they live like this?" Taryn said to herself. She knew she would have to start cleaning tonight, or Nathan would never hear the end of it from their parents tomorrow. As the older sibling, Taryn always took it on herself to cover for him when needed and step in to have those hard "parenting" conversations that Tiana and Noah never felt comfortable having with Nathan. This was just another one of those moments.

Heading from the bathroom back toward the party, Taryn took a quick glance at the boys' rooms and different dents and scuffs in the hallways. There were only a few areas they would need to fix and spackle, but the cleaning would be the death of them.

Slipping behind some of their friends, Taryn slowly made her way through the crowd and back with her bag. Once she made it to Nathan's room, she took off her jacket and placed it with the bag on his desk. Putting on some rubber gloves and her rubber slippers, she began to take out her cleaning supplies. Ajax, Clorox, Lysol, and a scrubber for the bathroom should do it for now.

In the bathroom, she organized her cleaning supplies on the cleanest edge of the counter. She folded all the clothes and towels she found in a pile that she placed on the outside of the door in the hallway, before organizing all their toiletries, toothbrushes, deodorant, etc., in the vanity cabinet.

She sprinkled Ajax all over the tile in the shower before standing on the ledge to spray Clorox on top of the Ajax from the top of the top of the shower to the drain. Letting that soak for a bit, she moved to the vanity and sink counter where she did the same Ajax-Clorox combo. Scrubbing the easiest area first, she loaded the toilet with Clorox and scrubbed until the porcelain looked brand-new, finishing it off with a coat of Lysol before wiping it down one final time.

Going back to the shower, she took off her rubber slippers and stepped inside. She began scrubbing from the top down, removing three years' worth of caked-on soap scum and calcium buildup. *Nathan owes me*, she thought to herself as she squatted down, scrubbing the bottom half of the shower to the drain. Stepping out and turning the water on, she stuck her feet in to rinse off the chemicals before leaning back in to splash water up the sides of the shower to rinse it.

"Why did I wear white?" Taryn said to herself, as she tried to hide behind the curtain in an effort to stay dry.

"I thought you're supposed to be drinking with all the college graduates?" a smooth, deep voice suddenly drifted over her shoulder.

Startled, Taryn turned quickly, tangling her feet on the tattered shower rug and tripping. She was suddenly falling backward, the shower curtain coming down around her waist and the cold water engulfing her face as she lay on her back staring up at the showerhead.

Derek

Derek had arrived at the party around 9:45 p.m., coming late from a cast-bonding dinner for the new Netflix series he would start filming next week. It only took him about five minutes sitting in a room full of young college kids to notice that Nathan's sister was not there.

"Hey, I thought you said older siblings had to be here?" he tried to ask Emma casually as he made his way across the living space to his sister.

"Yeah, well no one told you to come almost two hours late!" Emma said sarcastically. Noting her brother's face slightly drop, she added, "Maybe if you came earlier you could have had a drink with Taryn and prevented her from sneaking away to start cleaning."

"Cleaning?" Derek asked, confused.

"Yes! Cleaning!" Emma replied. "Nathan said she probably saw the mess of the apartment, since they haven't cleaned in a while, and when she didn't come back from her 'tour' of it, he assumed she started cleaning so he wouldn't get ripped by their parents tomorrow for being a slob. She always covers for him."

Not knowing what else to do, Derek nodded and grabbed a shot of soju that Reggie offered him.

"You should go find her. I think she's in the kitchen," Reggie added as he clinked glasses with Derek on a wink.

Sighing at the fact that he was caught looking for her, he drank his shot and headed down the hallway to look for the kitchen.

Sticking his head into the kitchen, the first thing that caught his eye was a sink of dishes that was soaking in soap and Clorox. She had to have already been in there, so he continued making his way down the hallway.

Peeking into the bathroom, he couldn't help but smile as he saw her. Standing maybe five feet one, she tippy-toed with determination to reach the top of the shower with gloves, spraying a bottle of Clorox in one hand, bracing herself on the shower wall with the other. Unable to help himself, his eyes scanned her body, taking in every inch of this woman he suddenly felt drawn to, not fully understanding why. He didn't even know her. But it was beyond obvious that he was highly attracted to her.

As she was balancing on her toes and the balls of her feet, Derek's eyes moved up toward her impressive, flexed calves that distinguishably protruded from the back of her legs. She had to have played sports or been an athlete to have calves like those. He didn't even have calves that were that nice. Moving his eyes north, he couldn't help but admire her behind. For an Asian, she had curves on her back there that could make any man drool—again, playing into the idea that she had to have been an athlete at one point or another. Her waist was slender as her thin white tank top seemed to hug her hips, hinting at a black lace bra lining the center of her back. With her arms held above her head, her shoulders and arm muscles were defined, toned, and tight but not bulky like those girls that lift weights. Her hair was pulled into a bun on the top of her head, revealing a tattoo on the back of her neck, going down her spine that appeared to be Japanese kanji, similar to the type of writing his mother had tattooed on her ankle. Even from behind, she was a truly gorgeous sight to take in.

As Taryn stepped backward out of the shower, pulling the curtain around in front of her, she leaned in to turn the shower on. Slowly, she began to splash water up the sides of the shower wall to rinse it, pushing her behind out toward the door right in Derek's direction. Although it was to try prevent herself from getting wet, the sight of her full, round behind right in front of his face was more than he could handle. It took all the strength in him not to reach out and grab it. Unsure of how long he was standing there staring, he shook thoughts from his head as he felt himself begin to swell inside the front of his pants.

"I thought you're supposed to be drinking with the college graduates? Not cleaning?" Derek tried to ask casually as he cleared his throat.

Taryn turned a little too quickly, Derek's voice seemingly scaring her, and Taryn twisted and tangled in the carpet then the curtain before she fell backward. Rushing into the bathroom, Derek stepped next to her, reaching around and into the shower to shut the water off, but it was too late. She was on her back, and she was drenched from her waist up.

"I'm so sorry," Derek said sincerely as stared down at a drenched Taryn, hands still in front of her face, half in the shower, half out of the shower. The black lace of her bra showing clearly through a now-transparent white tank top.

Minutes seemed like hours that passed as the two of them remained where they were, frozen. Derek was unsure if she was upset or mad, and he couldn't bring himself to move toward her either. So he just stayed there, staring down at Taryn with strands of her hair that escaped from her clip in the fall, matted wet to her face. Staring at the little droplets of water sprinkled around her face and on her lips somehow made Derek's heartbeat quicken. He swallowed hard. Her silence making it difficult for him to find words to say.

"Are you okay?" Derek asked cautiously. "I'm so sor—"

Suddenly Taryn burst out in laughter, cutting his apology short. Full, body-racking laughs seemed to take over her whole being. Her smile beamed up at him, and his heart skipped a beat, her laugh contagious. Stepping out and grabbing her hands, he slowly lifted her from the floor as they both continued laughing.

"Hi," she said with a bright, beaming smile between laughs. "We haven't officially met. I'm Taryn, Nathan's sister," she added ripping off her gloves, holding her hand out for Derek to shake.

"Hi." He laughed, shaking her hand. "I'm Derek, Emma's brother." This girl was something else, something he never expected.

Frozen in the moment once again, they stood there staring into each other's eyes as their hands moved up and down robotically.

Snapping out from what seemed like a trance, Taryn suddenly released his hand and shook her head, her smile faltering slightly as her body shivered.

"Damn it. It's cold," she said with a smile. "Forgot for a second that I just took an involuntary cold shower in fifty-two-degree San Francisco weather," she joked.

Moving past Derek toward the toilet, she grabbed a handful of toilet paper and began an attempt to pat herself dry. Derek couldn't help but laugh as he watched a trail of toilet paper pieces get stuck to her face as she tried to dry off.

"What's so funny?" Taryn asked wearily, unsure of what embarrassing thing she did now.

"You kinda got a little stuff stuck on you," Derek said with a smile as he vaguely pointed around his own face.

Touching her face, Taryn burst out in laugher again as she felt the bits of toilet paper. She could only imagine how ridiculous she looked.

"Here, let me help you," Derek suggested as he moved toward her.

Standing directly in front of her petite frame, at six feet tall, he seemingly towered over her. Gently, he began picking off the tiny pieces of toilet paper from her face as she froze, holding her breath. Slowly, his hand spread across her face and cupped her cheek as their eyes locked once again. Derek's heartbeat began to speed up again as his blood rushed down to his crotch. Searching his eyes, unsure of what was happening, Taryn bit down slightly on her bottom lip. Everything began to move in slow motion as Taryn felt the warm of Derek's breath get closer and closer to her face.

"Hey, you guys!" Emma's drunken voice snapped the two of them back to reality. "What was all the laughter about!" she asked as she emerged in the doorway of the bathroom. Reggie, Nathan, and Sienna popped their heads in behind her.

Derek and Taryn suddenly pulled away from each other and stood there awkwardly like two teenagers who just got caught by their parents doing something bad.

"I slipped cleaning your shower," Taryn stammered.

"Why do you look like a wet dog?" Nathan questioned.

"Um, when I slipped I tried to catch myself on the faucet and ended up turning the shower on…on myself," Taryn added, laughing, scrunching her face and hoping that her brother would believe her, knowing how clumsy she was.

"Classic Ti." Reggie laughed as he shook his head.

"How do you fit into her clumsiness?" Nathan turned his questioning eyes to Derek.

"I came to use the bathroom and saw her fall," he responded casually. "I was just helping her out of the shower when Emma here came in and scared us with her loud mouth."

"That's it?" Emma said, annoyed. "That's boring!" she added before turning, pushing past everyone and stomping back toward their party guests.

Everyone at the bathroom looked at each other with confusion.

"Classic Em." Reggie sighed before laughing and turning to find his girlfriend.

"You okay, Ti?" Nathan asked, turning his attention back to his sister.

"I'm good, actually I'm better than good," she said. "I haven't laughed like that in so long," she added, turning toward Derek, letting out another chuckle.

"Good to hear." Nathan smiled at seeing his sister showing sincere happiness for the first time in forever.

"Ti, use this to dry off," Sienna said, emerging with a folded green towel. "I promise this one is clean, I just washed it this past weekend." She laughed, looking with sass in her eyes toward Nathan.

"Thank you," Taryn said, grabbing the towel gratefully. "You guys go enjoy your party. We'll be there in a few."

Looking between Derek and Taryn one last time, Nathan nodded and then headed back to the living room with Sienna. Alone again, Taryn and Derek looked at each other before bursting out in laughter once again. They were the older siblings, but somehow their drunk younger ones were trying to act like the parents. It was ridiculous.

As Taryn began to wipe her arms, Derek's eyes were drawn to her breasts that perkily pushed themselves forward from beneath her clothing. Derek swallowed hard again as he stood in front of her, trying to keep himself calm as he began to pick toilet paper pieces from her hair.

Without thinking about how compact and tiny the restroom was, Taryn bent forward to wipe her legs, and her head inadvertently brushed up against Derek's crotch. Shocked by the unexpected contact, Derek jumped back and leaned forward to try and cover himself while Taryn stood up suddenly. With a solid crack, the hair clip at the top of her head connected with his jaw, and the two of them crumbled to the dirty floor in a messy pile of intertwined limbs.

"Now I'm the one that is so sorry!" Taryn said laughing as she held her head, looking up at him.

"I guess we can call it even now?" Derek said laughing, holding his jaw.

Staring at the beauty sprawled on the floor with him, half draped across his lap, a sense of calm contentment spread through his body, and he couldn't help but smile with pure happiness in his heart. Releasing his jaw, he gently brushed a stray lock of hair from Taryn's face and tucked it behind her ear, before caressing the side of her face with his index finger.

"I didn't scrub the floor yet," Taryn said suddenly, remembering, scrunching her face and thinking of the filth they were sitting on.

"We should get up then?" Derek asked, chuckling slightly as he nodded and looked around.

"I think that'd be best," Taryn agreed with a smile.

As they peeled themselves from the floor and began to dust themselves off with the towel, Taryn shivered again as she slipped her slippers back on.

"Damnit, I'm really soaked still," Taryn said, frustrated, pulling at the bottom of her tank top.

The soft tissue of her breasts peeked out with every tug at her neckline. Derek tried to avert his eyes.

"Here," Derek said, as he unbuttoned the black-and-gray flannel shirt he had over his black crew neck T and shrugged it off, handing it to Taryn. "Borrow mine so you don't get sick or freeze," he added with a nervous smile.

"It's okay, I can borrow one from Nathan," Taryn said sincerely, as she did not to want to inconvenience him.

She turned from the bathroom and headed to Nathan's room down the hall. Derek following behind her with his flannel in hand. Entering Nathan's room, Taryn opened one of his drawers and grabbed out a folded pocket T. Putting it to her nose, she gagged. He obviously didn't wear it in a while as it seemingly sat in the drawer absorbing the smell of old mothballs.

"Shit. Nathan took all the shirts he was keeping to the new apartment yesterday," Taryn said remembering. "No wonder why he didn't take this one. It smells like crap." She laughed.

Moving deeper into the room toward the desk, she opened her bag and realized the only clothes she had was a change of shorts, a sports bra, and her jacket. Her shirt for tomorrow must have fallen out when she was rushing to grab her things when she was packing. Holding up her sports jacket, she sighed, looking at the dry-fit material.

"You're not going to be comfortable in that," Derek noted, leaning against the doorframe.

"Yes, I am," Taryn argued.

"No, you're not. I have jackets like that to work out in. The material is meant to have no ventilation so you sweat," Derek countered. "Just stop being stubborn and use this please," he asked in a softer tone, holding out his flannel to her.

Taryn let out a heavy, defeated sigh and walked over to Derek, taking the flannel from his hand. He beamed with a bright smile, flashing his dimples at her and giving her a little wink.

"Can you at least turn around?" Taryn asked.

"Huh?" Derek responded, confused. He was unsure of what she was asking him.

"I know it's your shirt, but that doesn't buy you the right to see me put it on," she replied jokingly.

"Oh sorry," Derek said, turning around quickly, feeling embarrassed that she thought he wanted to watch.

He could hear shuffling happen behind him and the sound of clothing hit the floor. Derek's body began to heat at the thought of Taryn, shirtless, in that black lace bra he could see through her wet tank top, just behind him. Hands gently rested on his shoulder, and Taryn's breasts pressed into his back.

"It's safe now," Taryn whispered into his ear, her voice sending tingles down his spine.

Derek turned around and stared as she walked toward him wearing his flannel. She took his breath away, and he couldn't get words to come out from his mouth. Feeling his blood rush downward, he took a deep breath, calming himself.

"It was a little big, so I had to tie the bottom up a little bit. I hope that's okay," Taryn asked, unsure of herself, taking a step back so Derek could take a look at her.

"I think you should keep it," he said with a smile. "It looks better on you than it ever would on me."

Taryn blushed and dropped her eyes to the floor before walking over to Nathan's desk. Taking the clip from her hair, her dark-brown waves fell like a waterfall down her back and cascaded over her shoulders. As she turned back to Derek, her beauty hit him like a train, and he was speechless.

"Are you okay?" she asked as she approached him, rustling her fingers through her hair.

"Yeah, I'm just...yeah. I'm fine," he stuttered.

"Well, let's go get a drink before our 'parents' come back and scold us again," Taryn said sarcastically.

Derek nodded in agreement and held his hand out to her. Taking it, Taryn's fingers seamlessly interwove with his as if they were created to fit together perfectly. Smiling to himself, Derek slowly led her back toward the living room. His heart was beating rapidly in his chest, and his mind racing with wonder of what this woman stirred up in him in less than twenty-four hours. He never felt anything like this in his life, and the more he thought about the woman holding his hand, the more he felt drawn to her, giving him an adrenaline rush that no experience could ever compare to.

9

Taryn

"Finally!" Emma exclaimed as Taryn and Derek emerged in the doorway to the living space.

All eyes turned to the two of them. Taryn could feel her cheeks flush red but was unsure why. They didn't do anything wrong. Right? Nothing happened.

"You guys went oof?" Nathan asked with a frown, noticing that his sister was in Derek's flannel.

"No!" Taryn exclaimed. "My tank top was soaked, and none of the shirts in your room smelled clean or wearable. So Derek offered me his flannel," she explained.

After giving the them a hard stare, Nathan broke out in a smile and threw his head back laughing.

"Ha! That's right, my bad!" Nathan said. "All the clothes in that room either gotta be thrown in the trash or wash." He laughed. "But in my defense, no one told you to be clumsy when you're cleaning."

"Here you two, take shots. You guys gotta catch up to us." Sienna offered two shot glasses full of Hennessy to Derek and Taryn.

They looked at each other and accepted the glasses from Sienna. Clicking their glasses together, Derek and Taryn threw their heads back and allowed the liquor to burn down their throats, instantly spreading heat throughout their bodies.

"I guess that's one way to warm up after you take an ice-cold shower in the middle of the night," Taryn said to Derek, laughing.

Derek's face scrunched at the potent aftermath of the Hennessy shot and stared at Taryn in amazement once again. She barely flinched taking the shot.

"Do you need a chaser?" Derek asked Taryn, confused and slightly concerned.

"No," she replied, confused. "I'm okay." She laughed. "Do you need a chaser?" she asked him jokingly.

Being completely honest with her, Derek replied, "I might. That was rough." The two of them began to laugh again, completely oblivious to everyone else in the room.

"Fuck!" Nathan yelled, suddenly sending the room into complete silence.

Taryn and Derek quickly went into their concerned and protective older-sibling mode, maneuvering themselves through the crowd toward Nathan's voice. Pushing past a few more people, they found themselves next to a pissed-off Nathan, anger radiating from his body as he stared down the couch in their living room. The smell of vomit and alcohol was strong enough to make you gag. Sienna stood to the other side of him, rubbing his arm and trying to calm him.

"Nate, it's okay. It's just Chase. You know he doesn't know his limits," Sienna tried to rationalize with him.

"Yeah, bro, it hap—" Chase didn't finish his sentence.

Luke came pushing through with a trash can, but it was too late. Another gut-wrenching purge sent another waterfall of alcohol with chunks of unknown matter from Chase's mouth onto their couch. Luke's eyes grew large as he stared at Nathan, waiting for his explosive reaction.

"If you throw up one more time on the couch, bro, I swear I will force you to eat all your palu and then beat your ass and force you to hold that shit down!" Nathan threatened as he yanked the trash can from Luke and shoved it under Chase's face.

"Palu?" Derek whispered to Taryn.

"Palu. It's Hawai'i slang for vomit. Chase's from Hawai'i too, so he knows," Taryn whispered back.

Derek nodded. Taryn knew of Chase in general, the rich white party boy that sometimes hung around Nathan and his friends but always brought trouble when he did. But it still shocked Taryn that he was from Hawai'i. Chase did not embody any of the cultural aspects of respect, humility, and care for others that almost everyone in Hawai'i was brought up with. Maybe it was because his father passed when he was young, but that was no excuse to act the way he did in Taryn's book.

"Nate, calm down. It's okay. You guys start cleaning up the bottles and everything. I'll deal with him," Taryn said, trying to take the trash can from Nathan.

"Yeah, come on, babe. Let's start rinsing the bottles and cleaning up," Sienna added, supporting Taryn's plan to just get Nathan away from Chase to deescalate the situation.

"No! Fuck that! It's not okay! Where the fuck you supposed to sleep now? Not on the palu couch and not on the floor! And I'm too drunk to drive right now, so what the fuck!?" Nathan yelled at Taryn.

Squaring her shoulders and standing tall, Taryn's teacher voice took over. "First off, do not go swearing at me because your boy can't handle his alcohol. Second off, where I sleep is not a big deal. I can catch an Uber back to the other apartment. It's fine. And third off, you need to step the fuck back and calm down before I embarrass you and lay your ass out in front of all your friends," she said with absolute authority.

Everyone in the room got quiet and big-eyed, staring at the siblings. Nathan was the fighter in their group and was the one everyone called when they were in trouble because he wasn't afraid to throw down. Despite them never needing to because he was always so level-headed and chill, no one ever crossed Nathan because they knew the potential of his temper that brewed before that relaxed exterior.

Derek stood there next to Taryn, his hand finding its way to hers again, unsure of what else to do but hoping his little gesture could offer whatever support to her that she needed. Accepting his hand nonchalantly, Taryn still stood looking up at Nathan, their eyes locked in an angry death stare, neither budging.

"Fuck! Fine!" Nathan yelled, letting out a heavy sigh before dropping his eyes, putting the trash can on the ground next to Chase and turning to walk way.

"I love you, jackass!" Taryn yelled after her brother as a smile spread across her face.

"I love you too, stubborn bitch!" Nathan yelled back over his shoulder as he sauntered off, Sienna following in tow, beginning to pick up stray bottles. "Party's over, everyone. Put your empty bottles up on the table, take your trash out, and empty whatever beers you didn't finish in the toilet before you leave, or my sister is going to lick you."

"Shut the fuck up" Taryn yelled at him, laughing.

She turned her attention back to Derek; he was looking at her in utter confusion. She couldn't help but laugh.

"We understand each other. That's how we show each other love even if we disagree," she tried to explain to him.

"But 'lick' them? That sounds kind of gross," Derek said with slight disgust spreading across his face.

Laughing, Taryn continued, "Lick in Hawai'i is another slang. It means beat you up, fight you, etc."

"Oh," Derek sighed in relief. "That makes a lot more sense now." He laughed.

"Ti, I'm so sorry," Chase interrupted as he lifted his head from the trash can.

"It's fine. You just gotta realize you're young not that young anymore. You're graduating soon too, and then you're going to be in the real world, buddy. This shit won't fly anymore," Taryn told Chase in a sisterly tone.

Taryn knew that Chase was feeling bummed about not graduating with Nathan and the rest of their friends. Their sophomore year of college, Chase had gotten his heart broken by his high school sweetheart, and he went off the deep end pretty badly. He failed all his classes and got put on academic probation. Because of it, he had one more semester to go before he could graduate in the fall.

"Chase, take my towel, and I'll walk you down to the Uber we ordered for you." Reggie appeared on the other side of Derek, offering his help to Taryn.

"Thanks, bro," Chase said, taking the towel gratefully.

"I got him, Ti, thanks for cleaning the couch. Sorry again," Reggie said to her as Drew stepped in and helped Reggie get Chase to his feet before heading out the door.

Slowly, with Derek's help, they began to use the roll of paper towels Drew brought to them to push the vomit into the trash can.

"How are you not gaging?" Derek asked Taryn as he tried not to think about the sour spit that was filling his mouth and making him want to vomit himself.

"I've done this a lot," Taryn said with a laugh. "Every time I'm at gatherings like this, whether when Nathan comes home and drinks with his friends, or when I go to other house parties, I always end up playing 'mom' and taking care of the messy cleanups. I don't know why, but it just happens." She sighed.

"Don't need to clean-clean it, Ti. We were going to trash that couch anyways. It's fine. Sorry again," Luke interrupted as he grabbed the trash can from between them. "Thank you both, though. Appreciate it."

"Anytime. That's what older siblings are for, right?" Derek responded, nodding at Luke.

"It's part of our job description," Taryn joked.

"Shit, Ti. Sorry, you don't have anywhere to sleep now. Give me a bit, and I'll drive you back to Mom, guys, when I sober up a little more," Nathan said as he walked toward them.

"I can take her home," Derek offered sincerely. "I have to go back to my apartment anyways, and my dad's place you guys are staying at is just two blocks over. It's not a problem."

"It's okay, you guys, I can catch an Uber," Taryn said.

"I'm not letting you catch an Uber by yourself at midnight," Derek stated.

"Yeah, we're not letting you catch an Uber," Nathan added.

Nathan looked between Taryn and Derek for what seemed like an eternity before letting out a heavy sigh. He didn't know what was going on between the two of them, but he knew that something more than her falling happened in that bathroom. He just didn't want her sister falling for any guys if her heart wasn't healed yet.

"Derek, you sure you can take her home?" Nathan asked Derek. "Did you drink?"

"I had one shot of soju when I got here and one shot of Hennessy. I feel 100 percent fine, I promise," Derek said, seemingly not fazed being interrogated by a twenty-two-year-old.

"And you won't take advantage of her in the car?" Nathan asked seriously.

"Oh my gosh! Nathan! So inappropriate!" Taryn slapped her brother's arm, completely embarrassed. "Thank you for the offer, Derek, I'd really appreciate it," she said to Derek, trying to push past the awkwardness that Nathan just created.

"Don't appreciate it too much, if you know what I mean, Taryn!" Nathan argued.

Derek couldn't help but laugh at how protective Nathan was of his older sister.

"Nathan! Enough!" Sienna's voice pierced through the tension. "Sorry about that, guys. Good night," she said to Derek and Taryn. "Let's go to bed, now!" she said, turning to Nathan and yanking him from the living room.

"Good night," Derek replied.

As everyone began to clear out of the room, leaving the mess for the morning, Emma appeared out of nowhere, wrapping her arms around her brother's waist. She was wasted.

"Good night, brother. You're welcome," she said with closed eyes and a smile as she tilted her head in Taryn's direction.

"Oh my gosh. Good night, Em," Derek said as he peeled his sister from him and handed her off to Reggie.

"Night, guys, wash your hands before you go though. Vomit? That's kinda nasty," Reggie said as he picked Emma up and carried her to their room.

After washing their hands and grabbing her bag, Derek and Taryn found themselves alone, at midnight, on the sidewalk outside of the boys' apartment. The cold San Francisco air nipped at their faces as Derek shoved his hands in his pockets and Taryn crossed her arms as the air shocked her exposed legs. Walking a block over in silence, Taryn followed Derek to a black Jeep. He unlocked the doors and opened the passenger side for her to get in. She stood there and stared at him with a contented smile.

"What? Did I do something wrong?" Derek asked.

"No. Just shocked by your chivalry. It's not common nowadays," Taryn replied with a chuckle as she got in.

"Of course, ma'am" Derek replied jokingly as he bowed his head to her as he used his free hand to gesture her into the car before walking around and sliding into the driver's seat. As they pulled away from the sidewalk and into the night, Taryn felt at peace for the first time in months.

10

Derek

The glow of the streetlights kissed hints of warmth into Taryn's face as Derek drove through the sleeping stress of San Francisco. Replaying what happened in the bathroom in his mind, he couldn't help but smile. Even with the wonderful experiences his acting career had brought him, it had been years since he had laughed that hard or had that much fun in such a simple, sporadic moment. Slowly, more and more, he felt drawn to her far beyond the fiery attraction that first sparked his intrigue upon seeing her at the graduation that morning. It was as if every minute he got to spend with her had gained him months' worth of friendship, even if the only actual interaction they had was at the party tonight. He couldn't put his finger on it yet, but there was just something about her, a feeling that she was developing in him that he had never experienced before, and it was giving him the thrill of his life.

Glancing over at her sitting in the passenger seat, staring out the window, he couldn't help but smile to himself. *Damn, she was a little firecracker*, he thought to himself. She was tough, strong, and determined yet oozed kindness and empathy for others that he rarely saw in women his age nowadays.

"You can't really see the stars in the city, huh?" Taryn asked concerned, pulling him back from his thoughts.

"Yeah, between the fog and the city lights, the stars are typically hidden," Derek confirmed. "But on really clear nights and only if you're willing to freeze your butt off on the beach can you see some stars."

"That's one thing I'll miss about Hawai'i this summer," Taryn said, turning to Derek, sadness clear in her eyes that made his heart sink.

"What do you mean?" he asked, wanting to know more.

"Back home we live about a five-minute walk from the beach. Sometimes when I need to clear my head at night, I walk over to this spot on the beach, sit on the sand, and just stare up at the stars," she said, looking up to the sky, imagining it. "The twinkle of the stars on a clear night sky, the sound and smell of the waves crashing on the reef, and the feel of the sand between your toes." She sighed. "There's just something comforting about it all. I guess I need to find a new spot to clear my head this summer," she finished with a disheartened smile.

"I'm fairly new to the city still, and there's not anywhere like that that I know of, but I know a spot where you can clear your head and still get a pretty good view," Derek said. "I can show you really quick if you're okay with a little detour?"

"Surprisingly, I am," she said with a smile.

A few minutes later, turning down Turk Street, Derek found parking a little ways down from the bottom of Lone Mountain, the upper campus of the University of San Francisco. It was 11:50 p.m. already. They got out of the car, and Derek led Taryn toward the bottom of the famous Spanish staircase that led students up the front of the enormous hill and up to the north-campus classes.

"We're at the university?" Taryn asked, confused.

"Yes," Derek replied with a smile. "When we first moved Emma here and took a tour of the campus, I always thought the architecture of these stairs were breathtaking, and the views from the top are even better," he began.

"I felt the same way. This entire university is beautiful," Taryn said.

"In January, when I came to the Bay Area to film, I was going through a pretty dark time, and I would run to clear my mind. Most nights, I'd find myself running here and sitting at the top of the stairs, staring out at the city lights for hours just to feel a sense of peace again." Derek sighed, shoving his hands into his pockets as they began their trek up the stairs.

"I'm so sorry. If it's okay for me to ask, what happened?" Taryn responded, her voice drenched in concern.

"I've been off and on with my high school sweetheart Lexie, and right before the holidays we kinda called it quits indefinitely. She always thought my dream of being an actor was far-fetched and unrealistic. I was getting small parts here and there but nothing career changing, you know?" Derek said. "Before the holidays last year, she was fed up with me. She had just got her second promotion with the marketing company she worked for down in LA and left me for her supervisor."

"That's awful," Taryn exclaimed. "I'm not just saying that because I know you and not her, but that's wrong in general. The person you're with is supposed to be your partner. They are supposed to support you through good and bad, pushing you to be the best you can be and always, always supporting your dreams and aspirations."

"Thanks." Derek sighed. "But you know, the cheating wasn't what sent me into the dark place. It was what happened after."

Derek fell into complete silence as they made their way up their fifth flight of the Spanish stairs. Taryn, unsure of what to say or do, kept walking patiently in silence with him.

"I got the call that I got the part in the movie on New Year's Eve. I figured it be a great start, a fresh start to a new year," he began. "But the next day I saw that she had posted on her social media sites that she and her 'supervisor' got engaged." Derek scoffed as they stopped at the top of the Spanish stairs.

Taryn looked at him with empathy and slid her hand atop his forearm, caressing it gently in a show of support.

"It wasn't even two weeks from when she broke up with me, you know?" Derek said angrily. "My mind went crazy with questions about how long she was cheating on me for them to get engaged so quickly after our breakup. Like was she waiting for him to show commitment before leaving me? Was I just a backup? Was she waiting to see if I got famous or not before she decided she wanted to be with me? Would she had stayed if I were more success—"

Despite the cold, the warmth of Taryn's hands engulfed the sides of Derek's face, pulling him down toward her. Cutting him off before he could say anymore, her mouth hungrily smashed onto his. The warmth and softness of her lips melting him from the inside out, his breath caught in his throat. An explosion of emotions took over every inch of Derek's body as he wrapped his arms around Taryn, pulling her closer to him as if trying to make their two bodies, one. The kiss seemed to stall time for the two of them as the world and the problems in it rapidly fell away.

Suddenly Taryn pulled back, her persona totally changing, snapping Derek back to reality. Both of them breathing heavily.

"I'm so sorry," Taryn stammered. "I shouldn't have done that. Can we forget this never happened?" she asked as she quickly turned and began descending down the stairs.

"Taryn," Derek called after her as the wheels in his mind started functioning again after she just blew them to bits with that kiss.

For such a tiny person with short legs, man did Taryn move fast. It was like she was a professional at running away, which made Derek wonder if she was running away from her life too.

Once they were both on the sidewalk, Derek's long legs were able to finally make up the space between them, having to nearly break out into a run to catch up with her.

Grabbing for her hand gently, Derek asked, "Did I do something wrong? Are you okay?"

Stopping in her tracks, a few feet from the car, Taryn hung her head and replied, "No. I'm sorry. I just, I don't know. I've had a rough few months too, and I don't know what happened. I'm usually always in control, and for some reason it's like I have no control over myself around you. I didn't mean to cross that line. I'm sorry."

Derek stood in shock and silence, staring at the girl he saw: so strong and confident of herself all day, standing before him, now an unsure, self-questioning person. New questions began to form in his mind. What hurt her so bad in her past that she would suddenly seem so broken the second she was intimate with someone? Nathan said she had a rough year, and she just admitted to it herself. But what could have broken her to this point, and what else was her smile hiding? Whatever it was, it became like a magnet in that instant, creating a stronger pull to her than he ever felt to anyone before in his life. It may sound crazy after just one day of being around her, but he suddenly felt a need to comfort her, to fix her, to protect her.

11

Taryn

The car ride to the apartment she was staying at was full of complete silence. Taryn had not said a word since apologizing to him for the best kiss he had ever experienced. Derek remained quiet, unsure of what to say to comfort her and not wanting to push her any more than he already had.

As he pulled into the driveway of his father's apartment they were renting on Sixteenth Street in the Richmond District, the clock on his dashboard flashed 12:47 a.m. Derek parked the car and watched as she searched her bag for her key. Panic suddenly spread across her face as she searched again, and again. Looking ahead in a trance, she slowly closed her eyes and dropped her head back to the seat with a frustrated sigh.

"Fuck," she said quietly.

"What's wrong?" Derek asked.

"Nathan has the key," Taryn replied with a heavy sigh.

"He has your key?" Derek asked, confused, knowing his father gave each of them a key for the apartment.

"Nathan has his key. I gave my parents mine to use to get back in the apartment because they were going to go watch a movie tonight. I figured it'd be okay because I was going to be with Nathan so, I didn't need a key. Fuck," she said, her voice tinged with frustration at herself.

"It's okay, we'll figure it out," Derek said, trying to calm her.

"It's not okay," Taryn countered as she began to massage the stress from her temples. "The only way to get in is if I call my parents who are going to ask why I didn't stay at Nathan's place, who are then going to cuss Nathan out for letting the party get out of hand, which will cause Nathan to start a fight with me for ratting him out."

"I can take you back to get the key from Nathan if you want me to." Derek was trying to appease her.

"I wouldn't ask you to do that. I already feel like an inconvenience as it is, and besides, after Nathan and all of them drank like they did tonight, they are blacked out and won't answer my phone call anyways." Taryn sighed as she unbuckled.

"What do you want to do?" Derek asked, confused as to why she was getting out of the car if she was locked out.

"I'm just going to call my parents and make up some shit that I needed to come back but forgot to grab the key from Nathan. They'll be mad, but they're always mad at me for something, so it's nothing new," Taryn said with a sarcastic chuckle as she opened the car door.

Suddenly, Derek was reaching across her, grabbing the passenger door handle, pulling it closed.

"What are you doing?" Taryn asked, confused, and sitting back as Derek hovered over her, his hand still gripping the door handle.

"You're staying with me," he replied with a sigh and a sweet smile.

"Huh?" she asked, eyes wide.

"You…are…staying…with…me," Derek said again, emphasizing each word. "I'm not letting you get in trouble for being a good older sister, and I'm not going to get Nathan get in trouble either. My apartment is two blocks over on Eighteenth. You can stay at my place, and then I'll take you back to Nathan's in the morning before your parents get there," Derek explained as he reached over, grabbing Taryn's seatbelt buckle and clicking it into place.

Taryn sat there in shock, trying to process what just happened, what was happening. Why would he help to cover for her and Nathan? They just met. But before she could find the words to contest his offer, Derek was pulling into the street again. Seeing the uncertainty spread across her face again, Derek reached over the center console and took her hand in his, giving it a gentle squeeze to let her know everything was okay.

"It's fine, I promise," he said to her as he drove off.

Derek pulled into the driveway in front of a black garage door, driving in and under the building and parking it toward the back right of the compact garage. Reaching behind her seat, Derek grabbed her bag for her before gesturing for her to meet him at the front of the Jeep.

"This garage is pitch-black. How do you find your way through here at night without walking into things?" Taryn whispered.

"By walking into things over the past few months, I found out where to walk and where not to walk." Derek laughed. "But why are you whispering?"

"I'm not sure." Taryn chuckled. "I guess because it's late, and I don't want to wake your neighbors?"

"Don't worry, you won't. Most of them are businessmen that travel and are never here, so I typically have the building to myself," Derek said, jokingly whispering into Taryn's ear.

The heat from his breath sent a tingle down her spine, and she shivered despite herself.

"Come on, just follow me," Derek said, taking her hand into his and guiding her through the maze hidden in the darkness of the garage.

They reached the foyer of the building and took two flights of stairs up to his apartment that was on the third floor.

"You and your dad have a thing for third-floor apartments, huh?" Taryn teased as Derek unlocked his door, and they took off their footwear in the foyer.

"It's mostly my dad. This is one of his rental properties too. I'm just his tenant until August," Derek replied jokingly.

As the entered the apartment, she noticed that it looked like the splitting image of the one she was renting for the summer.

Seeing the confused look on her face, Derek explained, "Yeah, my dad remodels all his rental properties to look the same—same hardware, furniture, and everything. It's easier for him to buy everything in bulk and then simple to repair or get replacements later."

Continuing, he added, "But I rented this one-bedroom from my dad since it's just me."

Looking around the duplicate apartment, she saw that the layout was pretty much same without the guest bedroom or the secondary bedroom that Nathan and all of them were staying in at the other apartment. Derek's master bedroom was off the kitchen, with a dining space and living area flowing from the kitchen island. The dining table and sofa, just smaller replicas of the ones at her apartment. In the foyer, there was a little door that led to a mudroom-bathroom combo, with a full-sized bathroom and washer-dryer combo in it. The same sleek, modern style was detailed throughout the apartment.

Placing Taryn's bag on the island, Derek said, "You can come in, you know. I won't bite. I promise."

Giving Taryn a wink, he flashed that same bright smile that pushed joy into Taryn's heart all night. Taryn just shook her head and laughed to herself as she took off her slippers and walked to stand beside him at the island.

"Can I be honest with you?" Derek asked as he turned and leaned on his elbow against the island.

"Okay?" Taryn questioned.

"That was the first time in a long time that I've had an open, transparent conversation with someone. It felt really nice," he said, staring at her, his eyes seemingly looking into the deepest depths of her soul. "And honestly, I don't want it to end just yet," he finished, inching closer to her so their bodies were less than a foot apart.

"Neither do I. So here's what I'll do. I'll give you ten questions," Taryn stated with a sigh. "You can ask me any five, and I'll ask you five but there's a catch," she explained. "Whatever questions you ask, you have to answer for yourself first, and no matter what the question is, in keeping with the transparency, you have to answer the question and explain it fully."

"Pretty thick guidelines, Ms. Okata," Derek said, nodding, as if questioning whether or not he wanted to play her little game. "You run a tight ship, but I'm in. Anything to keep this conversation going." He smiled.

Giving her a sexy wink, he turned and walked to the other side of the island into the kitchen.

"Would you like a cup of tea?" he asked, pulling two white mugs down from a cabinet.

"Tea?" Taryn questioned. Most guys back home didn't drink tea, so his suggestion took her by surprise.

"Yeah, tea. I figured it's too late for coffee, and if I give you some hot chocolate, the sugar in it will have us up until morning," Derek stated plainly as he put a tea bag in each cup and began brewing hot water into a separate pot that sat under the Keurig on the counter.

Lighting the wood in his fireplace, he dimmed the lights as the flames began to kiss every inch of the living space with a warm glow and took a seat on his sofa, placing the tray with the teacups and hot water down on the coffee table.

"Well, come on now, let's get to these questions," he said jokingly as he motioned Taryn over and patted the cushion next to him.

Even if they had known each other as a mere acquaintance for less than twenty-four hours, she felt comfortable and safe alone with Derek in his apartment. Cozying up on the two-seater sofa next to him, she pulled her knees up to her chest, turning to him as he poured hot water into the cups and handed one to her.

"So," she said, sighing, "what do you want to know?"

"Ladies first," Derek countered.

Starting the conversation out lightly, she asked, "Why acting as your career?" Keeping to her own guidelines, she answered the same question in regards to her career first. "I chose teaching because I saw how one good teacher can have a lifetime impact on a kid, and sometimes you just need that person in your life. Where I grew up, I was lucky with parents, but for most of my friends and most of my students now, an influential teacher can be the most stable adult role model these kids have. I wanted to make a difference in my community through the kids."

Derek seemed to stare at her in awe, hazel eyes twinkling in the light of the fireplace, the brilliance of his smile embodying a warmth to it in the moment.

"Wow, that's inspirational and very selfless. I could never be a teacher. I don't think I'd be able to take responsibility for the lives of so many kids, let alone teenagers," he said honestly. "For me, I chose acting because I always loved seeing someone get lost in the story line of a good book. When you're acting it's like you bring that story line to life for an audience, and you see an array of emotions that make the long nights and early call times just worth it when the final product is shown. It's my type of art."

"That's so poetic," Taryn stated with admiration. "I give you credit for what you do because in order to make others happy with your art, you have to sacrifice a piece of yourself to every role. And to lose that sense of privacy to fans who suddenly think they know you by knowing your character? I wouldn't be able to do it."

"Well, I'm not 'famous,'" he joked. "But I didn't choose this career for fame and fortune, it's just my passion."

"Well, I'm glad you've found your passion. Not many are able to until it's too late," she said with a soft smile. "But enough about that, it's your turn."

Taryn braced herself for what question would fall from those beautiful lips of Derek. Watching him closely, she noticed that he was hesitating to ask what was going through his mind as he stared down at his teacup. His eyes suddenly looked anguished.

Taking a deep sigh, Derek dove right in.

"What happened this past year that made it so rough for you?" Derek asked, with sincerity and concern shadowing his eyes as he stared at her.

Taryn's blood drained from her body as she froze. Her voice caught in her throat. Her heart pounded rapidly as if trying to break free from her chest. Taryn wasn't sure if she was ready to open that door yet. She hadn't talked to anyone about it at all.

"Nathan mentioned to Emma when we ran into him at Target that you had a really rough year, that you won't even open up to your family about it," Derek continued.

Tears started to well up in Taryn's eyes as they began to search for an out, some way to escape the question.

"Taryn, you don't need to answer it if you don't want to talk about it, especially if you haven't even told your family anything. But take it from someone who has kept things bottled up before. It'll eat away at you until it destroys you." Derek suddenly changed his mind about wanting to know, seeing the clear discomfort that suddenly radiated from Taryn's body. "I'm sorry, I was out of line to ask that."

Derek turned away from her, placing his cup back on the table, and resting his elbows on his knees as he dropped his hand to his face.

Should I just tell him? Taryn thought to herself as she stared at this man who seemed to be mentally beating himself up for wanting to know the answer to a question she's been asked over and over again for a year: what happened?

12

Derek

I'm such a fucking idiot! Derek thought to himself. It was his first question, and he fucked it up already. Why couldn't he just start with something about Hawaii or her hobbies? He just *had* to do it, huh? *She hasn't even told her family anything. What made you think she was going to tell you, dumb ass?* His mind continued to put himself down.

A heavy sigh from Taryn pulled his eyes back to the now-fragile woman sitting on the sofa before him. Sitting up tall, taking a deep breath, and blinking hard to push back the tears that had fought its way to the surface moments ago, Taryn was suddenly composed.

"You're not out of line. You have every right to ask that question," Taryn corrected him softly. "You trusted me enough to open up about your ex back at Lone Mountain, and I appreciate that... The question you asked is very heavy for me to answer, and I'm not even sure where to start, to be honest," she added, looking down at the cup of tea in her lap.

"Taryn, you don't need to talk about it. I'm sorry." Derek tried to stop her, but it was too late. She had made up her mind it seemed.

"No, you're right. I have to face this sooner or later, and honestly the fact that you don't know my past, including my ex, makes it a little easier for me to talk about," Taryn said. "You see, my family loved him. My friends thought he was my soul mate from the moment we met. If I told any of them what happened, it wouldn't be okay anymore," she explained, tears glazing her eyes again.

She wasn't even full-on crying front of him, but seeing the hurt and pain she was feeling was more than his heart could take. Turning to her and resting his hands on her knees to show her the support she needed, he nodded for her to continue.

With a heavy sigh, she began her story.

"Toby and I met eight years ago after being set up by friends. We dated for a year before getting engaged and got married three years after that. Two years ago, right before our third wedding anniversary, I switched my birth control and began getting sick. My female cycles were completely thrown off, and my weight jumped up and down more than I can remember. My doctor ran tests on me, and eventually I found out that there was a 90 percent chance that I could never conceive and took me off my birth control. Knowing how much Toby wanted kids, my heart broke that I more than likely would not be able to give him the one thing he wanted more than anything else in the world. So I didn't tell him. That same year, I began an accelerated program to earn my doctoral degree in education, and as we began trying to conceive, I simply blamed my inability to do so on the stress from balancing schoolwork with teaching.

"Then about a year ago, on accident because he didn't come home one night and I tracked his phone, I found out he was having an affair. It was with one of his friends from his childhood, a female named Annalee that he was close with who was going through a divorce. And he always said he was just supporting her since she suddenly found herself being a single mom raising two kids. I didn't think anything of it, you know? I have friends that are guys that I grew up with too, that I'm close with, and we support each other. But we've never crossed that line, you know? But I guess in comforting her, he found comfort from our situation and his frustrations of us not being able to get pregnant. He found an instant family with her. When I found out and confronted him about it, he confessed and was beyond apologetic about everything, saying he would do whatever it takes to make it work between us and to fix our marriage. We went to counseling, we got new phones, he checked in with me wherever he went, all sorts of crazy stuff. And I never wanted to be 'that' wife, you know?" Taryn tried to explain herself as a stray tear rolled down her cheek, and she turned her eyes to the ceiling.

"Yeah, but he gave you a legitimate reason not to trust him. You were beyond justified in all that 'crazy' stuff," Derek interrupted.

"Thanks, but that's not the worst of it. Three months later, so about nine months ago, he sat me down and told me that Annalee found out she was pregnant and in her second trimester already. That it was his and he didn't know what to do because he didn't mean for any of it to happen." Taryn's voice began to tremble.

"What did he mean he didn't 'mean' for it to happen? He didn't mean to stick his dick in another woman while he was still married to you?" Derek was beginning to get angry at the thought of anyone hurting Taryn.

"Please," Taryn soothed as she took one of his hands in hers.

"I'm sorry." He sighed, frustrated, but understanding that she needed to get all this off her chest. And in order to do that, he needed to keep his anger in check and shut up.

Seemingly gathering strength to get the next words out of her mouth, Taryn finally confessed. "Toby was willing to stay with me, abandoning Annalee and his unborn baby to save our marriage."

Derek sat back in shock. If this Toby guy knew he fucked up and wanted to stay with Taryn, why aren't they still together?

"I filed for the divorce," she admitted as her whole body seemed to collapse on itself, her hands trying to catch her crumbling face as her body folded into her lap, tears finally flowing freely as if the dam she built to hold them back burst into a thousand pieces.

Not knowing what else to do, Derek maneuvered the cup of tea from beneath her, placed it on the table, and pulled her into his lap, cradling her as she sobbed.

"That's why everyone is so mad at me, because they think it's my fault our marriage ended. That I left him because I wasn't happy anymore. But they don't understand," Taryn choked out.

"If you tell them why you filed for divorce, anyone would understand that. You deserve to be happy," Derek stated, confused at why she was allowing everyone to be mad at her when she wasn't the one who ruined their marriage.

"You don't get it." Taryn shook her head. "I didn't end the marriage for me. I ended it for him."

Now Derek was really confused.

"One of my best friends in the whole world always told me, when you truly care for someone all you want for them is to be happy, even if that means they are happy without you," Taryn began. "I knew if I didn't do anything, Toby would have chosen to stay, but he would be miserable and end up resenting me for it, probably ending the marriage himself down the road after years of heated arguments and being filled with hate. If he wasn't miserable with me already, he wouldn't have turned to Annalee."

Derek began to understand what Taryn did.

"I filed for divorce because even if I knew it would hurt him in that moment, he would be happy because he would get everything he ever wanted in life with her," she said, tears streaming down flushed cheeks. "I couldn't give him a family. I couldn't even bring myself to tell him that. With Annalee he already had two boys, and then he had his very own kid on the way. Who am I to stand in the way of his happiness? If I really cared about him, I had no choice but to walk away so he could be happy," she finished on a whisper with a heavy sigh.

Derek was in utter disbelief at the selflessness of the woman he was holding. To put herself through so much pain and take the blame in silence for someone who did her wrong was something he could barely wrap his mind around. The strength someone would have to have to knowingly do that to themselves was unthinkable. It was downright insane. Now Derek was the one in shock.

"Hawai'i is a small state and O'ahu an even smaller island. Everyone knows everyone, and if everyone found out about what really happened, Toby wouldn't get the support he needed from his family to bring his first child into this world happily. So his family all thinks that Annalee helped him through our divorce after I just left him. That way they accepted her more. The only one who knows the truth is his mom because she's the only one that Toby doesn't keep secrets from," Taryn explained. "As for my family, well, I always got in trouble in high school so to have them mad at me for stupid choices isn't anything new. Besides, if they knew my cop cousins would probably find every excuse in the book to try pull Toby over and arrest him. We're kinda protective of our own in that sense back home," she tried to joke as she relaxed into his arms and leaned her head on his shoulder.

But what she went through and what she sacrificed for her ex was nowhere near close to being something to joke about. Lifting her face from the crevice of his neck, he stared into her eyes. He could feel his heart quicken as it pounded in his chest. Tilting her chin up toward him, he leaned down and gently placed his lips on hers in a simple kiss that fueled a deep desire and passion inside of him. Her lips were full and soft as he closed his eyes and tried to memorize the feeling of her lips, every tingling, electric sensation that her lips sent down his body. He could feel his heart swell in his chest.

Pulling back and looking her in the eyes, he whispered, "You are truly one of a kind, Taryn. How could anyone be so stupid as to ever let you go?"

13

Taryn

Who knew that simply talking about something could remove thousands of pounds of pressure from your shoulders? For the first time in over a year, Taryn's heart felt light. Resting her head on his shoulder hid her from the light of the fireplace, mentally exhausted from her confession. With the warmth of his body against hers and the strength of his arms as it encapsulated her, Taryn finally felt at peace.

Derek's finger found its way to her chin and pulled her face from its hiding place. Derek leaned forward, and his lips found hers, sucking the breath from her lungs and turning her into mush in his arms. The kiss lacked the aggressiveness like the one at Lone Mountain, but what fueled it seemed deeper—he was connecting with her soul beyond a lustful attraction.

Breaking the kiss, Derek's voice was drenched in sincerity as he said, "You are truly one of a kind, Taryn, how could anyone be so stupid as to ever let you go?"

Taryn swallowed hard as she stared back at this man, a stranger in retrospect, but someone who shattered the walls of security she built around her over the last year in less than a day. A man who jump-started the beat in her heart and could send waves of desire through her body, burning her stomach to her groin with just one smile.

Unable to avoid it much longer, she shifted herself on his lap, feeling him begin to swell under her. Maneuvering herself, Taryn turned to straddle him. His hands found their way from her knees, caressing up her thighs as they finally stopped on her bottom and pulled her closer to his body. Resting her hands on his shoulders, she slowly moved them up his neck to rest at the base of his nape. They were staring in each other's eyes, both unsure of whether or not they wanted to cross that line. Both were gripping onto each other as if to brace for whatever was to happen next. Their heartbeats were pounding, breath heavy as they seemed to remain frozen in that moment.

"How long has it been?" Derek asked as he tried to control his breath as the bulge in his pants continued to push against the material that prevented it from connecting with her.

"What?" Taryn asked between breaths tinged with desire. Her eyes, glazing over, filled with need. It had been too long, and she was beginning to lose control, becoming overwhelmed with pent-up desire.

"How long since you last slept with someone?" Derek asked. The thought of him being the first man she may be with since her ex-husband made him feel uneasy for some reason.

"Eighteen months. My ex stopped touching me after he found his built-in family," Taryn stuttered, insecurity in her eyes.

Her breasts were heaving just below his line of sight, and his need to touch them was growing with each second. But he didn't want to do push if she wasn't ready.

"Taryn," he said seriously, sinking back into the chair.

"I'm sorry." She sighed with embarrassment, covering her face with her hands. "This was stupid."

Taryn began to lift herself from his lap.

"No, it's not like that." Derek smiled as he gripped her hips and pulled her back on his lap, having her sit down. "Look, I want this just as much as you do, if not more… Trust me. It's been awhile for me too, but you're vulnerable right now, and I just don't want you to feel like you have to. We don't have to do anything, and you don't need to 'give' yourself too because I said something that was true. I wasn't trying to just get in your pants." Derek's voice was drenched in sincerity.

Sitting back into his hands and dropping her hands to his chest, she stared at him in confusion. Did he think he was taking advantage of her? Was she taking advantage of him? Taryn had no idea what was going on, but the desire pulsing through her veins and the growing burning sensation in her abdomen were beginning to cloud her judgement.

Tucking a strand of hair behind her ear, Derek explained, "When I said you were one of a kind, I meant it, and I don't want to rush whatever this is between us if it is as special as I believe it may be."

He sighed heavily, trying to calm his own longing to lose himself with her before continuing.

"I want to, Taryn, I do. I want to feel every inch of you. But not tonight. I know I feel something between us, but I don't want to rush it just because we were both emotionally vulnerable from a night of confessions." He smiled as he pulled her face close to his so their noses were touching. "I don't want anything more from you tonight than your company," he finished, pulling her to his chest and wrapping her in his arms.

Taryn sighed and smiled despite herself. Derek's impact on her was stronger than she realized, and it blew her mind that she could have such a strong connection to someone she barely knew. Sitting up and wrapping her arms around his neck, she pushed herself against his chest as she leaned in and kissed him lightly on the nose.

Derek reciprocated and planted a gentle kiss on his right dimple before moving his lips all across her face, showering her with affectionate kisses. With each, she could feel him pulse beneath her.

"Thank you," she whispered into his ear before giving a soft kiss on his cheek. She could feel Derek smile against her face.

Suddenly, she was lifted from the couch, his arms creating a seat for her under her behind as he stood up carrying her. Guiding her legs around his waist, Taryn smiled as she wrapped her arms around his shoulders.

"What are you doing?" she giggled.

"Respecting you," he said as he pulled her in closer to him, kissing her cheek as he walked into his room toward his en suite.

FALLEN

Sitting her on the counter, Derek nudged himself between her legs, hands resting on her hips. Tilting her head to the side, her brown waves cascaded over her shoulders, and she gave him that same smile that made his insides melt. Turning from her, he turned his shower on and began running the warm water for her.

"Jump in," he said, gesturing with his head toward the shower. "Get all the Clorox and soap off you from when you fell cleaning the boys' shower, and I will be back in a few. I'll go put the tea away and put out the fireplace," he added, kissing her on the nose.

As Derek left the bathroom, Taryn stripped down, thinking about how crazy this entire night had been. Nights like tonight were only supposed to happen in novels, and those "too good to be true" movies. How was this even real? Was it just not being intimate with anyone for eighteen months that was putting her hormones in over-drive? Was it being in San Francisco? She never did stuff like this back home.

But it was different with Derek. She couldn't explain it, but it was. He made her feel safe and comfortable, a level of peace set-tling in her soul that she never thought she would experience again. She never knew it was possible to actually connect with someone so deeply in an instant like she did with Derek, and it was an adrenaline rush like no other.

Stepping into his shower, she was amazed. His shower was as big as her entire bathroom back in Hawaii. At the entrance, a white quartz bench stood with two columns of jets lining the wall behind it, a separate knob to turn them on. Smooth gray and black stones were placed like puzzle pieces on the floor, massaging her feet as she walked on them. Looking up, a huge showerhead was releasing water in soft raindrops, the steam rising as the warmth of them hit the cool tile stones. Across of the bench two more showerheads were fixed on the opposite wall, the lower of the two with a handle to detach it.

"His water bill must be ridiculous if he uses all these. Who needs so many ways to shower?" Taryn said softly to herself.

She was so amazed at the elaborate shower that, between her own thoughts and the sound of water falling from the rain shower-head, she didn't even notice Derek come back into the bathroom.

"I don't need all these ways to shower, but my dad overthinks, and he figured the more options the better," Derek said, smiling at her as he leaned against the entrance to the shower by the bench. His eyes were taking her in.

"Wha—" Taryn said, spinning around quickly, and again for the second time in one night with him slipped and fell onto the ground. Her back met the cold, wet tile with a thud.

Derek was suddenly by her side. His basketball shorts and a white crew neck T-shirt he had changed into, suddenly soaked from the rain shower as he knelt down next to her. He snaked one hand behind her head to get it off the hard ground as he draped an arm across her stomach until his hand rested on her waist.

"Are you okay?" Derek asked, totally unconcerned about her nakedness or his clothes being drenched. His brown curls matted wet against his forehead. His eyes seemed to stare into her soul. He was breathtaking.

"You need to stop sneaking up behind me like a ninja," Taryn said jokingly as she burst out into laughter, resting her head back into his hand as the water from the showerhead continued to pour raindrops down on her, kissing every inch of her skin.

"I'll try to walk louder," he said sarcastically with a smile.

They both broke out into laughter as they sat there, face-to-face next to each other, just laughing.

The pad of Derek's thumb inadvertently began to rub the small dip in Taryn's waist. Her breath catching under his touch, Taryn's eyes drifted up the length of his body. Every inch of muscle in his chest, abs, and shoulders transparent through his soaked shirt. Propping herself up on her elbow, Taryn ran her fingers up his wrist, slowly tracing every dip in his muscles up to his shoulder before running across the length of his chest and resting at the base of his abdomen. Her eyes following the path her fingers created. His body trembled with each movement as he struggled to control his breath as she explored him. Dropping her eyes lower, seeing a bulge clearly growing in his pants, Taryn's breath caught in her throat as she bit down on her lip to control herself. Without thinking, Taryn slipped her finger into the waistline of his shorts, his muscles tensing under her touch as she tugged the elastic of his shorts.

Shifting his body, Derek's arm that was resting on her waist was suddenly wrapped around her back, his other hand slipped moving from her head to grasp the nape of her neck. His body leaning over hers, the water from the rain shower was falling around him as he took her mouth with his. His tongue slipping past her lips with longing, as if it were searching for something beyond that moment.

Taryn's hands shot up, grasping at the sides of his shirt, before finding the seam at the bottom and running her hands on the bare skin of his back. His solid, toned muscles tightening, seemingly in sync with the movements of his tongue. Reaching his shoulders, Taryn pulled him down, closer until his body pinned hers to the floor.

With her heart racing and desire to be even closer to him, she dragged her nails down his back, pressing him into her. Sitting the both of them up, the rain from the shower falling between them, Derek pulled off his shirt in one smooth motion. Taryn's eyes at seeing his chiseled body in its entirety almost knocked her back down. Not wasting a moment, Derek leaned against the shower wall, pulling Taryn onto his lap and paused for a moment, taking her all in with his eyes. His hands started exploring her body as his chest began to heave with anticipation.

Derek leaned forward as his hands slipped to her lower back and pulled her toward him. The softness of his lips landed between her collarbone as he showered her with kisses. Taryn's hands shot up to grasp his shoulders as her head fell back, sounds of pleasure falling from her lips as she clenched her eyes shut. Her body began to tingle for him as their bodies slipped against one another from the wetness of the shower. The suspense was killing her already. She needed him now.

"Derek, forget respecting me. I need you...now," Taryn breathed heavily into his ear as she pulled his head up from her breasts. "Please, I want you," she pleaded.

Sitting back, staring at her, trying to control his breath, Derek nodded. With her still wrapped around his wet torso, he managed to hold her to him as he peeled them both from the shower floor. Turning off the water, he walked toward the counter, placing her on the towel he pulled from the rack nearby.

Bracing herself up, gripping the edge of the counter, she watched him as he pulled off his soaked basketball shorts, letting himself spring free. Her eyes grew big, and her mouth began to water as she bit down on her bottom lip, her heart beating fast with anticipation. Derek was smiling at her as he took in her reaction at seeing him in his entirety. Her entrance was wet and waiting for him.

"You sure about this?" Derek asked with sincerity as he nudged his way back between her legs slowly, bracing his hands on either side of her on the counter.

Unable to find her voice, Taryn just nodded as she stared into his eyes, her arms wrapping around his neck. Her hands pulled his face toward her, their mouths finding each other once more. In an instant Derek gripped her behind with one hand, pulling her toward him as her legs instinctively wrapped around his waist, his other hand bracing her back up, yanking her chest onto his. Without breaking their kiss, he walked back into the room and placed her gently on his bed.

As he hovered above her, he gently slid a knee between her legs, prompting her to move up toward the headboard with him. Once her head found the softness of the pillows, Derek used his other knee to push her legs open as he nestled himself between them, his hardness resting on the inside of her thigh. Leaning over her, Derek placed one hand on either side of Taryn's head, bracing himself. As she glanced at his forearms, she could see his muscles and veins bulge through his skin as his face strained as he tried to control the tension within him.

His mouth crashed into hers as their tongues moved together in a dance of passion. Derek propped himself up on one elbow, his shoulders tensing. Pulling back, Derek slowly brushed a stray hair from Taryn's face as he stared down at her. Lust filled in her eyes, her breath almost erratic. Cupping her cheek in his hand, Derek slowly lowered himself onto her. Taryn could feel him hovering at her entrance, teasing her, building the anticipation and tightening her muscles. As he stared into her eyes, he slowly dipped his hips forward, filling every inch of her as she gasped for air. The warmth and tightness of Taryn hugged every inch of him, squeezing him, pulling him into a deep abyss of euphoria.

"Derek," she moaned as her hands shot to grip the bedsheets beside her, every inch of her body clenching around him.

"Don't do that," he breathed heavily as he smiled at her.

"Sorry," she said innocently. "I didn't mean to. I told you it's been a while."

Steadying himself, he tried to relax as he allowed her to adjust to him. Derek leaned down, pressing the full weight of his body onto her as he begun to gently kiss her, his hands exploring her body as he began to move his hips. Plunging himself into her depths caused the tension in Taryn's stomach to build, that familiar burn in her lower abdomen threatening to release. Frantically, Taryn gripped onto his shoulders; she was almost there.

"Derek," Taryn moaned, her muscles tightening on the edge of her release. "Don't stop."

Derek picked her up from the bed, his hands guiding her legs around his waist as he walked back into the shower. His was still buried inside her. Her arms wrapped around his neck as she surrendered to him. Turning the rain shower water on, the heat filled the bathroom with steam. Sitting on the bench in his shower, he began pumping up, into her. His hands were running up and down the length of her back, moans escaping from their mouths between passionate kisses. Gravity sinking him deeper.

"Together, Ti," Derek said as he pushed her up against the cool tile. He could feel the muscles inside of her begin to twitch as she ran her hands through his wet brown waves before resting on his shoulders. With a roll of their hips, their mouths colliding, Derek let out a moan as he filled her, his entire body tightening and shaking. The feeling of his release pushed Taryn over the edge as she dropped her head to his shoulder, her release causing every muscle inside of her to tighten and tingle, her body shaking uncontrollably with pleasure.

As they relaxed into each other, their muscles tensed slowly as they rode out their pleasure together. The only sound was the shower drops hitting the tile. With the steam growing thicker around them, Derek tilted Taryn's chin up so he could see her face.

"Hi, beautiful," he said as he kissed her nose.

"Hi," she sighed with a chuckle.

"You are amazing," he replied as he wrapped both arms around her waist, pulling her closer, resting his chin on her chest.

"Why, thank you," Taryn replied jokingly. "You're not so bad yourself." Taryn kissed him on the forehead as she wrapped her arms around his neck.

"Can we just stay here forever?" Derek asked.

"Come on," Taryn said with a laugh as she slowly lifted herself from his lap, turning toward the water cascading down from the ceiling.

"No, just stay here," he argued as he pulled her back by her waist and onto his lap.

As she sat on his lap, Derek hugged her to him, resting his chin on her shoulder.

"I don't know what this is between us, Ms. Taryn, but if this is what twenty-four hours is like with you, I can't wait to see what adventures time will bring into our lives together," Derek whispered to her as he kissed her on the cheek.

Taryn smiled despite herself. She finally felt happy, but was it too good to be true?

Derek

That was the best sex he had ever had. He wasn't sure if it was because he'd thrown himself into his work so much that he didn't even have time to be intimate with anyone anymore. But whatever it was, he was blown away. The more time he spent with her, the more time he wanted with her, and now after tonight he knew he needed her in his life. But was either of them ready for what they just started? Did Taryn even feel the same way?

As he stood there, playing with her casually in the shower as they shampooed and scrubbed each other, Derek's heart felt light and he had a yearning inside of him to be closer to her. After creating an ice-cream shaped sculpture of soap atop her hair, he smiled and laughed to himself as he stared down at Taryn.

"Everything okay?" Taryn asked with a smile.

"Yeah, sorry. I guess I'm just zoning out," Derek replied.

"Considering how busy we've been in the last few hours, I'm pretty sure the sun is going to rise in five minutes," Taryn joked.

As they rinsed off, Derek made sure to pull her close and shower her with kisses, unsure of what would happen when they'd leave the confinement of his apartment. After wrapping himself in a towel, he turned to help dry Taryn off.

"I can wipe myself down, you know?" she said sarcastically.

"I know but you just gave me the best night of my life. The least I can do is take care of you," Derek replied with a wink.

Laughing to herself, she threw her hands up in surrender as she let Derek go about drying off every inch of her body, giving extra attention to her breasts with a few extra squeezes.

"Gotta make sure you squeeze all the water out," he told her.

Taryn couldn't help but laugh at his silliness and the fact that she was so comfortable around him so soon.

Derek picked her up, cradling her in his arms as he walked her back to his bed. He laid her down on the sheets before pulling the covers up and tucking them around her.

"Am I not allowed to put some clothes on?" Taryn asked with a sly smile.

"Okay," he sighed, "if you insist." Derek opened one of his drawers and pulled out a black T-shirt, tossing it onto the bed for her to put on.

Derek stood there, covering his eyes.

"What are you doing?" Taryn laughed, confused.

"I'm being a gentleman and giving you some privacy to get dressed," Derek said innocently.

They both broke out in laughter, as Derek dropped his towel and pulled on a pair of boxers before climbing into bed next to her.

"So you wear the underwear and I wear the shirt?" Taryn said casually. "Together we are one partially clothed person." She laughed.

"Exactly." Derek sighed as he wrapped an arm around her waist and pulled her close to him.

As they lay there, Derek couldn't help but think of how perfect their bodies fit together. It felt right to hold her close to him, and before he knew it, they were both fast asleep.

*****

"Shit!" Taryn said suddenly as she shot up next to Derek in bed, looking at her phone that was faintly vibrating.

Derek looked over his shoulder at his alarm clock sitting on his nightstand. It was 9:45 a.m. already. They were supposed to be back at the boys' apartment by 10am.

"Hello?" Taryn asked casually, trying to push the sound of sleep from her voice.

"Ti, where the fuck are you? Mom guys called and said they'd see 'us' soon. I'm assuming you never made it back to the apartment, and you are obviously not here, so where the fuck are you? I can't cover for your ass if I don't know where the fuck you are!" Nathan's voice rang over the phone and Derek could hear the concern in her brother's voice from the other end of the bed.

"I'm with Derek," she confessed.

"Wait, what?" Nathan replied, confused.

Seeing the anguish on Taryn's face, pulled Derek up beside her. It was as if she were some irresponsible teenager that had just been caught sneaking out of the house. Derek wrapped an arm around her waist. Thankful for the comfort, she leaned back onto his chest as she sighed and continued.

"Yeah. He was going to drop me off to the apartment when I realized that Mom guys had my key, because they went to the movies and you had the other key," she said casually. "I didn't want to wake anyone, so Derek offered me his couch since he was going to be coming by today anyways to help Emma and Reggie pack too."

There was a long silence on the other end of the phone line. Taryn's faced scrunched up, as if preparing to be yelled at by her younger brother.

"Nate, it's Derek," he said, as he pulled the phone from Taryn's hand.

"Did you sleep with my sister?" Nathan asked bluntly.

Looking to Taryn for what answer to give, she frantically shook her head, eyes wide.

"No. We didn't do anything, Nathan," Derek countered.

"Well, then, why are you guys waking up so late? Unless you guys stayed up late doing shit," Nathan argued.

"Nathan, we just talked all night. We lost track of time and fell asleep on the couch," Derek tried to ease Nathan's mind.

"You fell asleep on the couch? Together?" Nathan's voice seemed to raise with each inflection of his tone.

Standing up in frustration, Taryn yanked her phone back.

"Do not go in on Derek! If anything, he saved your ass because if I had woken Mom guys to open the door, I would've had to explain what happened at your party last night that prevented me from sleeping there." Taryn's tone was of full authority. "If I had called you last night, you wouldn't have answered because your ass was that drunk. So it was either get you busted, sleep on the street, or stay at Derek's," she added in a huff.

Nathan fell silent, his breathing heavy through the phone.

"Look, Nate, Derek is a good guy who was doing something nice for his sister's friend's sister. Last night was nothing, not a big deal at all," Taryn emphasized.

Hearing those last words sank Derek's heart. Last night was a big deal for him. He would never admit it to anyone, but his heart felt full just being around her. Was it really nothing to her? Did she see their night together as just casual sex? It wasn't for him, and he wasn't sure how to deal with it if she didn't feel the same. Especially since this was the first time he felt this way about anyone. Sliding out of bed, Derek moved silently toward his closet and got dressed. The sound of Taryn's voice was merely a whisper in the background of his thoughts.

"Okay. Just be careful" Nathan sighed, giving up.

"I promise," Taryn replied. "You know, you gotta stop this thing where you act like the older sibling now. It's not cool," she said sarcastically.

"Well, when you grow up and learn to communicate with me, maybe I won't have to," Nathan countered. "I'll just tell mom then that you and Derek went on a coffee run for all of us."

"Thank you, Nate. We'll be sure to stop and grab coffees on our way to you," Taryn replied before hanging up.

Derek emerged from the bathroom then, toothbrush in his mouth, eyes saddened.

"You okay?" Taryn asked as she approached him, going to place her hands around his waist.

Derek just shrugged her off, pushing her arms down before turning back into the bathroom. Taryn was hurt. What brought on this sudden mood change?

"Here," Derek said, handing her a toothbrush before walking out.

He was suddenly cold and off-putting. His thoughts about her conversation with Nathan consuming him. He knew she felt something too last night. Not just their sexual chemistry but something deeper, an emotional connection that he couldn't have just imagined. But was she really so damaged by her ex that she would never admit it to herself? Again, was last night really just nothing for her?

Emerging with a frown from his room, her bag in hand, Derek looked at the beauty standing before him. Even without makeup on, even after only a few hours of sleep, she was still stunning. His heart skipped a beat before dropping completely, thinking that their connection would be confined to just that one night they shared.

"You ready?" Derek said as he rose from the sofa, grabbing his keys and jacket by the door.

Taryn just followed his motions silently, unsure of what to say or what she did to make him change his mood so suddenly.

"We'll stop at Philz on the way and get coffee for everyone," he said as he opened the door. "I heard you and Nathan's cover story," he said with a glance over his shoulder.

"Thank you," Taryn said silently, hurt clear on her face.

It killed Derek to act the way he was acting toward her. He wanted to just hold her hand, wrap her around him, and be with her again, but the hurt from his past prevented him from doing that.

The ride to Philz and to the boys' apartment was completely silent. Derek, wanting to break the tension multiple times, couldn't find the words to do so. The wall of protection that he had torn down was suddenly taller than ever around Taryn. He had pushed her to silence again, and Derek was beyond mad at himself for that.

As they pulled into the boys' driveway, Emma and Reggie were throwing away some of the big boxes the boys had in the rented dumpster.

"Hey!" Taryn said to Emma, her mood suddenly changing, that smile back to shield the world from what she was feeling inside as they pulled into the driveway.

"Hey!" Emma replied with a sly smile as she opened Taryn's door and helped grab some of the coffee cups from her.

"Taryn," Derek said softly. "Maybe just leave your bag in my car until later. So your parents don't see you bringing it with you into the house. You wouldn't bring a whole bag like that on a coffee run, that's why."

Taryn just nodded with a smile. The tension between the two of them clear to Emma and Reggie who stood watching the awkward exchange.

Smiling at the two of them, Taryn headed up the stairs.

"What the fuck did you do?" Emma said slapping Derek on the arm.

"What?" Derek asked confused.

"I'm not stupid" Emma argued. "I saw that, whatever that was," she added, motioning a hand between Derek and the stairs where Taryn disappeared to.

"It's none of your business," Derek said.

"It is my business if you messing with Nathan's sister is going to get your ass beat up," Emma countered.

Taryn was like an older sister to Reggie and he stood there like a rock, arms crossed behind Emma, waiting for Derek to explain.

"Look, she slept over last night because she didn't have keys to the apartment. We talked all night. That's all," Derek said, exasperated.

"Liar," Emma said, after taking a long, hard stare at her brother. "I know you, Derek, and I know I haven't seen that spark in your eye since you and your bitch of an ex first started dating. My question is why, despite that spark, is your body language depressing and Taryn is suddenly all fake-happy again? What the fuck did you do?"

"It's not me, okay? We did talk all night. I opened up to her about shit I haven't talked to anyone about, and vice versa." Derek sighed, frustrated.

"Wait, she opened up to you about the divorce?" Reggie interrupted in shock.

"Yeah, she did. I don't know why, but she did. We had a genuine connection last night, you know," Derek said with awe, thinking back to his time with her.

"But?" Emma pushed.

"But it meant nothing to her. I heard her tell Nathan this morning that last night was nothing, no big deal," Derek said as he hung his head. He knew how it artificial it sounded, saying it out loud, but it didn't make the words hurt any less.

"D, you know she probably said that because she's not ready to explain jumping into anything with you yet?" Reggie tried to reason. "If she couldn't even talk with her family about her divorce, how odd would it be for her to suddenly be talking about her night with another dude?"

"I guess you're right." Derek sighed.

"Wait, if you're the one that felt hurt by what she said, just so she didn't have to explain herself just yet, why was she the one that looked more so hurt?" Emma questioned.

"Um…" Derek couldn't bring himself to say how much of a jerk he had been all morning.

"Derek!" Emma questioned angrily.

"I might have ignored her all morning, brushed her off, pushed her away when she went to hug me, been fully cold toward her," Derek said guiltily.

"Derek! What the fuck is wrong with you!?" Emma yelled, throwing her hands in the air, almost dropping the cups of coffee.

Derek just hung his head.

"You gotta talk to her, man. If she opened up to you about her divorce, keep in mind you are literally the only person she's ever talked to about it, and that means something. It may not seem like a lot, but for Taryn it was a lot. She doesn't ever concern other people with her problems or how she's feeling, so for her to feel safe enough with you to open up, it's a big thing. You gotta fix this," Reggie said.

"You're right. I'm a fucking idiot." Derek sighed.

"Yeah, you are!" Emma snapped. "Go talk to her now!"

Once in the apartment, Taryn had already thrown herself into cleaning again. She had different piles organized for what they were keeping, what they were donating, and what was trash.

"Hey, D," Nathan said curiously.

"Hey, Nate," Derek replied. "Have you seen Taryn?"

"Why?" Nathan questioned.

"I just gotta talk to her," Derek said.

"Look, I don't know what actually happened between you two last night, but she seemed genuinely happy hanging out with you, and the fact that she defended you on the phone is pretty big. Don't fuck with her or hurt her, okay? I'm fine being homeless this summer for kicking your ass if you do," Nathan said bluntly.

"I promise. She's been through it, and I would never want to be the cause of any hurt she ever feels," Derek replied.

"Wait, what do you know about her going through it? What did she talk to you about?" Nathan asked, confused.

"She opened up to me about what happened with the divorce." Derek sighed.

Shock covered Nathan's entire face as he seemed to lose any ability to speak. *Taryn talked about her divorce?* Nathan thought to himself. Unable to say anything else, Nathan just nodded.

"She's in the kitchen," Nathan surrendered.

"Thank you," Derek said, giving Nathan a smile before heading toward the kitchen.

"Hey, seriously though, please don't hurt her. She has the biggest heart, and I can't stand to see her break down like that again. Okay?" Nathan added, before heading back down the hall toward his room.

"Ti?" Derek said cautiously as he entered the kitchen.

Taryn was standing on the counter, checking the expiration dates on the food and tossing them down into the different trash bags sprawled on the floor.

"Taryn?" Derek said, a little louder as he knocked on the wall near the door.

Still she gave no response. He really did hurt her.

"Taryn, can we talk please?" Derek asked as he approached the counter and rested a hand on her calf.

Startled, Taryn slipped on the spare trash bags next to her on the counter. She was falling to the ground quickly, but this time Derek was swift. Catching her on his chest before stumbling back toward the ground cradling her, he caught her before she could hit the floor.

As he lay on the ground, still holding her body toward him, Taryn's breath caught in her throat. The warmth of his body penetrated through the icy facade she tried to hold on to.

"Uh? You guys okay?" Luke's voice carried toward them from the door.

Looking up suddenly, Taryn quickly pushed herself up from Derek, pulling earbuds from her ears and leaving him on the floor feeling utterly empty.

"Yes, I just slipped on the counter, and he caught me," Taryn said, brushing herself off.

"Ti, you are so fucking clumsy." Luke laughed. "I don't know why we trusted you to climb up onto a high counter to clean."

"Well, I'm okay now. I just can't stand on slippery plastic trash bags," Taryn said jokingly.

"All right. Well, let me know if you guys need help in here," Luke said before turning to head back down the hall.

"Taryn, will you just talk to me?" Derek said, peeling himself off the floor, walking toward her as soon as he was sure that Luke was out of earshot.

Placing the earbuds back into her ears, Taryn reached for her phone on the counter. Holding it up so he could see it, she turned the volume to its max. Lifting a leg up and placing her foot on the counter, Taryn began climbing back up to finish her cleaning. But before she could, Derek's hands were on her waist and spinning her to sit on the counter facing him.

"Now you want to talk?" Taryn said angrily as she pulled the earbuds from her ears.

"Yes, please," Derek pleaded with her.

"Okay, so talk," she said shortly. Sass radiated from her, full force, as he stared in shock at her sitting before him.

"I'm sorry," Derek began.

"Hmm. Sorry for what? Sorry for being a typical guy, having sex with me when I was vulnerable? Sorry for pretending to actually care? Sorry for having me confess the sins of my divorce to you only to be cold about it the next day? Or sorry for even taking me home and putting yourself in that situation to begin with?" Taryn shot at him.

Stunned, Derek was shocked into silence.

"Hmph," Taryn said. "That's what I thought. Look, it's whatever, honestly. I just can't deal with people that I trust enough to confide in, being fake to me. So we'll call it like it is. Last night was fun, but it is what it is. It was just sex. Nothing more, nothing less," she said coldly.

Derek could do nothing but stare as Taryn continued.

"It was actually my fault for opening up to you, and it was my fault because I pushed you to fuck me. So you know what? I'm sorry. I'm sorry for opening up my heart and my legs to you. You don't need to apologize for anything," she finished. "Hello? You there?" she asked sarcastically as she snapped her fingers in front of his eyes.

Is that why she was upset? She thought I was using her vulnerability for sex? Derek thought as he stared aimlessly at the coldhearted, hurt girl he had held in his arms less than a few hours ago, now sitting before him.

"I don't have time for this. Thank you for last night, but whatever we felt or thought we felt, it was a facade," Taryn said as she hopped down from the counter, her front sliding down him as she got down.

Instinctively his arms shot up and gripped the counter, one on either side of her, trapping her in front of him.

"Taryn," Derek sighed, unable to say anything else as she stared at him, waiting for him to say something, anything.

Bending down and slipping out from under his arm, she pushed past him, shaking her head as she walked out of the kitchen.

"Fuck," Derek said, frustrated, as he pounded his fist onto the countertop.

15

Nathan

Almost slamming into his shoulder, Taryn rushed past Nathan in the hallway, headed straight to the door.

"Ti! You okay?" Nathan asked, concerned.

"Yeah," she urged. "I just need some fresh air. Some of the old food in your pantry was giving me a headache. I feel nauseated."

"Okay. Well, Mom guys are patching up holes in the living room. Maybe we can take a break when they're done and grab lunch," Nathan suggested.

"Perfect. Sounds good. I'll be back," Taryn said quickly as she rushed out the door.

Suspicious of his sister's behavior, he headed toward the kitchen where he found Derek, a frustrated mess standing over the sink.

"Derek? You good?" Nathan questioned.

"No," Derek sighed heavily.

"What's going on?" Nathan asked, concerned.

"I think I fucked it up with Taryn," Derek confessed with his head hung.

"Wait, what? How did you fuck it up when nothing even happened yet?" Nathan asked.

"Yeah, why don't you tell Nathan how you fucked it up, you big dummy!" Emma's voiced echoed from the doorway with her hands on her hips.

"I was feeling insecure about my own feelings for her after spending the night together, and I kinda pushed her away," Derek summed up.

"You pushed her?" Nathan exclaimed, stepping forward with fists clenched at his sides, anger radiating from every inch of his body.

Derek took a step backward, hands in the air in surrender. Emma and Reggie rushed in. Emma grabbed her brother's arm, Reggie stepping in between the two men.

"Not physically, Nathan. I would never put my hands on her or any girl like that," Derek explained. "After hearing her tell you last night meant nothing to her on the phone, I started to brush her off and ignore her."

Nathan's chest began to rise and fall rapidly, nostrils flared as he stepped forward again.

"It was stupid of me to do because I was hurt at the thought that I was imagining the connection we had," Derek continued. "Nathan, in one night I have developed feelings for your sister that I have never felt for anyone in my entire life. I don't even know what I'm feeling, but I do know that whatever it is between us, I need her in my life. The thought of losing her alone makes my heart ache. I would never intentionally hurt your sister. It was all a big misunderstanding, and I just need her to talk to me, so I can explain myself," Derek pleaded.

Nathan looked between everyone in the room, Emma's eyes pleading with him to give Derek a chance. Reggie, his trusted friend, rested a hand on his shoulder.

"He's a good guy, Nate," Reggie said.

"Don't make me regret this," Nathan said after a long pause, holding his hand out to Derek to shake.

"I promise I won't," Derek replied, shaking Nathan's hand before pulling him into a bro hug.

"Okay, now that that's settled, what can we do to help?" Emma said, eager to see her brother happy.

With that, Nathan called Sienna and the other boys into the kitchen and began developing a plan to get Taryn talking to Derek again.

"What was all that about?" Tiana asked Nathan as everyone moved into the living room. "Is Taryn done with the kitchen?"

"No, we had some rotting food in there that made her sick, so she went for a walk to get some fresh air," Nathan replied.

"Hi, I'm Derek. I'm Emma's brother." Nathan watched as Derek held out his hand to Nathan's parents.

"Hi. I remember you from the graduation yesterday. You're the actor, right?" Tiana said with a smile.

"Yeah, that's me. You guys raised two wonderful human beings," Derek stated to them.

Tiana and Noah looked at each other in confusion before turning their attention back to Derek. Nathan was beside himself, trying not to laugh at the awkward moment transpiring in front of him.

"Thank you," Noah replied cautiously.

"He has the hots for Ti!" Luke yelled from across the room.

"Thanks, Luke," Derek said, embarrassed.

Tiana and Noah's faces dropped to the floor as Derek's face turned bright red as he cowered before them. It took everything in Nathan's power not to burst out laughing, but he felt for Derek. He knew his parents were tough, so he swooped in to help.

"He's the same age as Ti, Mom. He saw her cleaning the bathroom last night instead of partying with us, so he opted out of drinking and helped her instead. They got to talking all night and just hit it off," Nathan explained, as he squeezed some reassurance into Derek's shoulder.

"Oh," Tiana said. "Well, thank you for helping her. It's nice to hear she's socializing again. It's like she's been living under a rock since her divorce."

"Tiana," Noah said with big eyes, nudging his wife in the arm.

"Shit. Did she not tell you she was divorced?" Tiana began to panic.

"No, it's okay. She told me all about it. She's so strong for being able to push through after everything that went down. She's amazing," Derek said.

"Wait, she talked-talked to you about the divorce? She didn't just say she got a divorce? She actually opened up to you about what happened?" Noah asked, shocked, as Tiana was stunned into silence next to him.

"Yes, she did," Nathan answered for him. "Which I'm happy about, don't get me wrong. It's good she's talking about it. But it's just fucked that she opened up to you, barely knowing you before she opened up to us."

"What the fuck!" Taryn's voice pierced through the current conversation as she stood in the doorway.

"Taryn," Derek gasped.

"I told you that shit in confidence. I told you why I couldn't tell anyone else, and you're out here fucking blabbing everything to Nathan and my parents? For what? To get on their good side because you were a fucking jerk-off this morning? Fuck this shit! I'm out," Taryn said as she turned and stormed out of the room.

"Taryn," Derek repeated as he made his way toward the door.

"Just give her a few. Let me talk to her first. It'll be okay," Nathan said, halting Derek in his tracks.

"Ti!" Nathan yelled. "Yo! Ti!"

His sister's only way around the city was him or Uber. She didn't know how to catch the Muni, and the Bart was nowhere near the boys' apartment so he knew she couldn't have gotten far. Walking down his street and a block over to the park, he saw her sitting on the swings. He walked over to her and sat on the open swing next to her.

"You okay?" Nathan asked.

"No," Taryn replied. "I can't believe he told you guys everything. I was going to tell you. I swear I was. It was just easier talking to him because he didn't know my situation. He didn't have an opinion on Toby, so it was just simpler." Tears glazed over her eyes, threatening to burst forward.

"Ti, I get why you talked to him. I just wish you would open up to us, or at least to me, so I could assure mom and all of them that you really are dealing with it all okay," Nathan said, his voice drenched with concern. "And if it makes you feel better, he just said you two talked. He didn't give details."

Taryn stopped swinging and looked over at her brother. She could tell by the look in his eyes that he was telling the truth.

"Fuck. I'm such a bitch," Taryn said with a sigh.

"Yeah, you are. But you had good reason to assume, and now that he fucked up this morning and you fucked up five minutes ago, you guys can call it even," Nathan said with a smile.

"Shut up," Taryn laughed half-heartedly.

"But seriously, Ti. What happened with you and Toby? You don't gotta tell me everything, but I need to know. It's killing me to know that little facade you're putting on and potentially hiding serious pain. I don't ever want you to end up like Dougie," Nathan stated.

Dougie was Taryn's childhood friend. They grew up together, and he was always there to care for her when Nathan was still just a little kid and couldn't. Dougie was always smiling, happy, everyone else's rock when they went through tough times. But behind his smile was pain. A pain that no one knew about until he hung himself. It was the worst day in Taryn's life, knowing that he took his life because he was suffering alone on the inside and not talking to anyone about the shit he was going through.

With the reference to Dougie, Taryn let out a heavy sigh and said, "You're right."

They sat at the swings, rocking back and forth for almost an hour as Taryn poured her heart out to Nathan, telling him every detail and event that transpired leading up to the divorce. Instead of being angry like she expected him to be, he was understanding and listened to her without interrupting. She answered every question he threw her way and now understood why she didn't want to tell their family members. He too knew how they could be, and with Hawai'i being such a small state, it would be hell on earth if anyone found out what truly happened between her and Toby.

"I get it, Ti. I do. The only thing that bothers me is you taking the blame for him and letting everyone be pissed at you when he fucked up," Nathan finally said when she was finished.

"I know. It bothers me at times too, but it's easier this way, you know? He needs his family, and if they knew the truth, he wouldn't have anyone anymore. Our friends would even turn on him, and right now, with the new baby coming he needs that support." Taryn sighed. "Besides, I'm tough and I've dealt with haters all my life. It's nothing new. Just taking it day by day, trying to find new reasons to smile."

"Well, I gotta hand it to you. You are tough. I don't know if I could ever be the bigger person to that extent. You really are awesome, sis," Nathan said with admiration.

"Thanks." She sighed. "But while we are confessing stuff, I wasn't 100 percent honest about last night with Derek," she added hesitantly.

"You fucked him, didn't you?" Nathan asked, shaking his head with a laugh.

"Don't judge!" Taryn laughed. "It's been a really long time. Didn't you hear the Toby story? Eighteen months!"

"Okay. Eeew! I don't need to know," Nathan said, covering his ears. "Just be careful, okay. Don't rush into anything until you're ready for real. He legit got feelings for you."

"What?" Taryn replied in shock. For some reason that didn't make her feel any better. If anything, it scared the life out of her.

"I don't know what happened, and I don't need to know, but he told all of us that he had a legit connection with you and felt stuff he'd never felt before in his life," Nathan ratted.

Taryn was shocked. After this morning, she truly believed he was only saying those things last night to get in her pants. It worked and it was amazing, but she wasn't even sure if she was ready to feel what she was feeling again.

"Earth to Ti?" Nathan said, snapping her from her thoughts. "Look, like I said don't rush it. Just know that he does feel some type of way about your guys' 'connection' last night," he added mockingly.

The two of them laughed together as they took a few more pushes on the swing before getting up and walking back toward the apartment.

Everyone had gone to finish packing in their rooms or meet with their own families for dinner. Sienna saw them approaching from the window and met them in the driveway.

"You okay, Ti?" she said as she pulled Taryn in for a hug.

"I feel a lot better now," Taryn replied.

Nathan smiled at two of the three most important women in his life, supporting one another. He was beyond ecstatic that Taryn had liked Sienna.

Tiana and Noah made their way down the stairs, closing the door behind them.

"So you're a little slut, huh?" Tiana asked jokingly with big eyes.

"What?" Taryn replied in shock.

Everyone broke out laughing at Tiana's forwardness. Their family was so close that talking to each other bluntly like that was just second nature.

"Let's go get dinner." Noah pulled everyone back from their momentary lapse of insanity.

"Can we go back to the apartment? Do Olive Garden on Uber Eats?" Taryn asked, needing a simple night in after the craziness of the last twenty-four hours.

"Sounds perfect," Tiana replied as they began to pile into Sienna's car.

Grabbing Nathan's arm to keep him back for a second more, Noah asked, "Your sister okay?"

Now knowing the full truth, Nathan replied with confidence, "She will be."

16

K-Elements

Beep beep beep beep beep.

The alarm on her nightstand went off at 8:00 a.m. Taryn, rubbing sleep from her eyes, sat up and reached for her phone. A part of her was hoping for a text from Derek, but then she realized they never exchanged numbers. Setting it down, she began to stretch, searching her room for her bag so she could throw her dirty clothes into the wash.

"Fuck," she sighed as she let her body fall back into the pillows. Her bag was still in Derek's car. Derek, who was probably pissed at her right now for accusing him of talking about her divorce when he really didn't.

Knock knock knock.

"Hey, Ti, Sienna has her last final today, and I just got called into my office for an emergency meeting," Nathan said as he popped his head into her room.

"Okay. What do you need?" Taryn asked.

"Can you do me a huge favor and cover my shift at K-Elements? The yakiniku restaurant I work at on the weekends?" Nathan asked innocently.

"Wait. If you only work there on the weekends, why do you need a shift covered today?" Taryn replied.

"Because it was supposed to be Sienna's shift, but I took it from her since her final got moved to today, and now I can't because I gotta go to a meeting downtown for my real job," Nathan explained. "Come on, Ti, please? You were a badass waitress back home. This will be cake for you!" Nathan pleaded.

"What about Mom and Dad guys?" Taryn asked.

"We got them tickets to ride the double-decker tour bus in the city as an early birthday gift for Dad, remember?" Nathan reminded her.

"Shit, that's right." Taryn sighed. "Ah, okay. I'll cover your shift. Your manager is okay with that?"

"Yes, Sienna will be okay with that." Nathan laughed. "I'll drop you off there in an hour before I head to my meeting, okay? Thank you!" he shouted over his shoulder as he turned to leave her room.

*****

It had been five years since Taryn put on a waiter's apron and worked in a restaurant, but she had done it so long when she was in undergrad that it was second nature to her already. After Nathan's coworker Chris briefly went over how to do things, Taryn went to work. She was quickly able to get into the swing of things, smiling at her own ability to adapt on the fly.

Customers came in, she greeted them with waters and appetizers, then put their order in for which meats they were going to cook. Every now and then, she had a grill-change request from the customers. But Chris was amazing and always beat her to it, so she didn't have to risk burning her arm as she was short, and it was difficult for her to reach across the table. Waitressing again was so fun, and she was considering seeing if Nathan could get her a job here on her off days from the university this summer.

"Ti, we got a bigger party, ten top in the back room," Chris said. "They wanted privacy and requested Nathan, so you take it since you're the closest to Nathan that they can get," he added jokingly with a wink.

"All right, I got them," Taryn replied as she walked over to the back room.

"Welcome to K-Elements! My name is Taryn, and I will be your server today," she said with a bright smile as she approached the table.

The eyes of the young men and women at the table suddenly turned their attention to her. *I thought this was a ten top? Why are there only nine of them?* Taryn thought as she scanned their faces and smiled at the ethnic diversity sitting before her. Other than Nathan's group of friends, she had not seen diverse groups of people in the Bay Area. A lot of times, when they went places, people seemed to drift toward their own race. Seeing a table with Asian, African American, white, and Indian individuals mixed in together made her truly happy and reminded her of home.

"Hi," a beautiful Indian girl with dark black hair and bright eyes said to her. "I'm Ananya," she said with a smile, holding her hand out.

"Nice to meet you," Taryn said as she took Ananya's hand and shook it.

"Can I start you out with some drinks?" Taryn asked.

"I wish we could drink right now, but we're only on lunch break," a Hispanic man with long curly hair tucked under a backward baseball cap said with anguish. "Damn, we should have come here for dinner instead after we were done filming!"

"I'm so sorry, I meant anything to drink. I can get waters for the table. We have sodas, and I can make some fun virgin drinks if you can't consume alcohol right now," Taryn tried to reason.

"Don't mind him," Ananya said, taking control of the situation. "We've just had alcohol at every one of our cast-bonding events that's why it's not a problem. Waters for the table will be fine."

"Perfect. I'll get the waters and your appetizers. Take a look at the menus and see what meats and veggies I can bring out for you folks," Taryn said before turning on her heels and heading toward the kitchen.

*****

"So is that her?" Ananya asked excitedly, turning her attention to the opposite end of the table once Taryn was a good distance away.

"Bro? Are you trying to hide from her?" Ben laughed as he took off his baseball cap and twisted his hair up with a rubber band.

"Yes, that's her, And no, I'm not hiding," Derek said, sitting up and leaning onto the table to talk to his castmates.

"You were hiding," said Jared sarcastically as he looked over his shoulder to Derek who was sitting next to him. "And just so you know, you and I are the same size. I'm pretty sure she saw you trying to slouch behind me."

"I wasn't hiding," Derek insisted.

"Okay, so that's the girl you were talking about all night yesterday?" Jared said, trying to ease his friend's obvious tension.

"She seems really nice," Ben added.

"Well, guys, we're here to ask her the hard questions that Derek is too chicken to ask. We're not just castmates, we're a family, and we gotta make sure she's not crazy," Ananya said.

"Please don't," Derek pleaded.

"If you're not going to talk to her, D, we will," Ananya argued.

Derek dropped his head. He couldn't stop thinking about Taryn after she stormed out of the living room yesterday. He felt horrible that she thought he told people about her divorce and even worse that she thought he only said those things to sleep with her. Despite the odds with only knowing her a short time, he truly grew to care for her, and her opinion of him mattered.

At the cast-bonding dinner last night, everyone could see he was bothered, and he ended up rambling on about her all night. He had been in touch and getting to know his castmates since he got the part two months ago, so when they saw he wasn't his normal, happy-positive self, they were concerned. Then, when they found out it was over a girl, after knowing about how his last and only relationship had ended, their intrigue over Taryn grew.

Everything was going according to plan, though. Nathan made up the story to get Taryn to take his shift, and Derek was here like he was supposed to be, in a setting where she had to talk to him. He just wasn't sure how it was going to go with his castmates wanting to ask her 101 questions now. This would be an interesting lunch hour. For a tiny, sweet person she scared the wits out of him. Derek continued to peer out of the room, watching Taryn work, and searching for a way to gain the courage to face her.

*****

"Hey! Welcome to K-Elements! I'm Tar—" Taryn was cut short in her greeting as she approached a smaller table of four people just outside of the back room.

"Ti?" the lean man with tattoos going down his arm exclaimed, a little girl sitting next to him.

"Lewis?" Taryn said, totally surprised. "Look at you! Successful military man in the flesh. You look better than you do in your Instagram posts," she finished, a huge smiling beaming from her face.

As Lewis got up, Taryn walked around to the other end of the table to meet him. They embraced each other in a huge hug, Lewis lifting her off her feet and giving her a little spin.

"Oh my gosh! How long has it been!?" Ti said as he placed her on her feet.

"Almost ten years I think," Lewis replied. "Wait, what are you doing in the Bay?"

"Nathan graduated this past Sunday, and he had to go to his other job today. I'm just filling in, so I didn't have to third wheel on Mom and Dad's day date," Taryn explained.

"I see, I see." Lewis smiled. "Where's your husband?"

Taryn's face dropped as she suddenly grew uncomfortable. Unable to explain to her old friend, she simply held her left hand up. Grabbing it and looking at her finger for a ring, Lewis's brow furrowed in a frown as concern grew across his face.

"What happened?" Lewis asked in a serious tone.

"It's a long story, but we finalized it about six months ago," Taryn said with a sigh.

"Why didn't you call me?" Lewis said. He was clearly upset.

"Lewis, you have your own life up here. I see you thriving, and we haven't talked since I got engaged. It would've been awkward just calling you out of the blue like, 'Hey, how you been? I'm divorced by the way,'" Taryn replied sarcastically.

"True," Lewis scoffed. "But we grew up together. Even if we haven't talked in a while, you still could've called. I still got you," he added, pulling her into another hug as he rubbed her back and kissed the top of her head.

"Thank you, Lewis, I appreciate that," Taryn said, squeezing his waist as he held her to him.

"We gotta catch up, so give me a call this week, okay?" Lewis said, looking down at her. "Anyways, you remember Tyson and Kyle, right?" he said, nodding toward the other two men sitting at the table.

"What? Yes! Of course I do!" Taryn exclaimed as she released Lewis and stood behind the two men, throwing her arms around their shoulders and pulling them into a mini group hug. "What are you guys doing here? Don't you two still live in Hawai'i?"

"Good to see you too," Kyle added. "You know, we were still friends, and when you lost touch with dummy over here, you could've kept in touch with us," he said jokingly.

"Hey, Ti. Ignore him as usual" Tyson laughed. "Yes, we do, but we missed our boy here so we took a week's vacation to come and help him redo the flooring in his house," Tyson went on to explain.

"And who is this beautiful little girl?" Taryn said, turning her attention to the child sitting next to Lewis. The child was sitting in a pink outfit with lopsided pigtails, smiling.

"This is my daughter, Kamryn," Lewis said, sliding back onto his chair next to a beautiful little girl. "Kam, this is Aunty Ti. Can you give her a hug?" Lewis said gently to his daughter.

Taryn's heart filled with joy for Lewis and sadness as she knew she would never be able to call someone her daughter. Moving her eyes between Lewis and Kamryn, she couldn't help but smile.

"Hi, sweetie!" Taryn said as she squatted down next to the table.

"Hi," Kamryn said in a tiny voice as she wrapped her arms around Taryn's neck and hugged her.

Taryn wrapped her arms around Kamryn's waist and lifted her up, carrying her.

"She is too sweet," Taryn said, a smile trying to hold back the tears that glazed her eyes.

Placing her back on the chair next to Lewis, Taryn wiped her face and shook off the emotions that were threatening to take control of her.

"All right, all right. This is too much," Taryn said with a laugh. "Let me get you some drinks, and I'll bring out the appetizers in a few, okay?" On that note, she turned to walk away.

Lewis beamed a smile after her, completely smitten, as Tyson and Kyle looked between them, shaking their heads.

Watching the interaction between Taryn and this mysterious tattooed man, Ananya was suspicious. When Taryn walked away from their table, she leaned toward the door in an attempt to listen in on their conversation.

"Ananya, what are you doing?" Ben asked, laughing.

"Shhh! I can't hear them," she said.

"Ananya, stop!" Derek emphasized.

"She knows these guys, maybe they know something about her that you should know, just be quiet!" Ananya argued.

"Just leave it alone!" Derek retorted.

Ananya ignored his pleas and listened intently to the conversation. She couldn't make out everything they were saying, but she was getting bits and pieces of their conversation drifting her way.

*****

"See?" Tyson said to Lewis.

"See what?" Lewis said as he sat back.

"If you had just told her how you felt back then, maybe things would have been different for both of you," Kyle said bluntly.

"What are you talking about?" Lewis said.

"Don't act. You can't fake it with us, bro. We know you," Tyson said seriously. "That year she was single, before she met her, well, ex-husband now, you guys got really close."

"Yeah, we all thought you were going to end up with her," Kyle added.

"We were just friends." Lewis laughed.

"Friends my *A-S-S*," Tyson spelled out.

"We know you got feelings for her. How could you not? Ti is awesome" Kyle said. "And…we know you guys hooked up a handful of times toward the end," he added, whispering across the table.

"It doesn't matter. Feelings or not, hooking up or not. She didn't see me that way. She made that very clear when she started dating Toby," Lewis said with a heavy sigh.

"Bro! She did have feelings for you! We all saw it! And Ti isn't the type to just hook up with someone casually. She was just waiting on you to grow some," Kyle argued.

"Things happen for a reason, though." Lewis sighed. "If I had made a move to be with her back then, I would've messed it up anyways. I wasn't mature enough yet, and I was selfish. Maybe if I learned to care about others sooner, me and Kamryn's mom would still be together. But look at how that turned out? Even after maturing, six years after Ti, I was still dumb. And now I'm taking care of Kamryn on my own," Lewis added, smiling down at his daughter watching her iPad.

"Well, if things happen for a reason, there is a reason you ran into her today. Keep that in mind," Tyson stated.

Lewis reflected on how happy he was that year hanging out with Taryn. He had just moved back to Hawai'i to finish college and was a waiter at the local Chili's when she came in with her friends for dinner. She had just gotten out of an abusive relationship, and her girls were trying to get her out of the house. Lewis remembered how her beauty shone from across the room and took his breath away. It was the first time he had seen her since they were in middle school, when she would be at her uncle's house next door to his with her cousins. After exchanging numbers that night, they were inseparable. They would study together, grab dinner, and binge-watch movies on the weekend at Jack's house. They became best friends and more.

On his birthday that year, he was sick and she came over to cook dinner for him. As she cared for him that night, tucking him in, he pulled her close and crossed the friendship line, placing a kiss on her lips to show how appreciative he was of her. From there, things just happened. He made love to her for the first time that night, and it was the best he had ever had. She blew his mind and couldn't believe he was lucky enough to be able to have that intimacy with her in addition to their friendship. But despite their growing intimacy as time passed, he couldn't bring himself to confess his feelings to her. He believed that if he told her how he felt, she would leave. After his own mother left, Lewis always dealt with his fear of abandonment.

His heart broke when he found out she was dating Toby. In his mind it validated everything that he believed, that she was going to leave him, that the possibility of more than friendship was all in his mind. He couldn't open his heart to her again.

*****

Looking around, Chris helped to bring all the tables their waters and appetizers. He saw her catching up with Lewis, and since the restaurant wasn't too busy yet, he helped her out. Taryn had to just go back to the tables and put in their orders for different meats for them to grill.

"Thank you so much, Chris, for helping," Taryn said sincerely.

"No problem! It's nice to be needed," Chris replied jokingly.

"Chris, you are awesome!" Taryn replied with a smile.

"Girl, with that smile, I'd help you hide a body if you needed me to," he said with a wink.

"Oh stop," Taryn replied, giving him a playful nudge on the arm. She was truly appreciative of Chris taking him under her wing on such short notice for Nathan.

"I'll go greet the next table for you. Just go get the food orders from the back room and your friends," Chris encouraged.

"Okay. Thank you again, Chris!" Taryn said as he went to the front to greet more customers.

"You guys ready to order?" Taryn asked as she approached the ten top in the back room.

"Who's that guy?" Ananya asked with a casual smile, pointing to Lewis's table.

"Oh, that's Lewis. He's a friend from back home. Haven't seen him in forever, though," Taryn said.

"Why?" Ananya questioned.

"We lost touch after I got engaged. Not sure why, though," Taryn answered. "Um, what meats and veggies can I get for you?" She tried to change the subject.

"What? You're engaged! Well, probably married now, right? Congratulations!" Ananya said enthusiastically.

Derek shot daggers across the table with his eyes at Ananya as he slouched behind Jared. He had already told them last night that she was divorced.

"I'm actually divorced," Taryn said quietly.

"Oh, I'm so sorry. What happened?" Ananya continued.

"It's kinda personal. Did you guys get a chance to look at the menu?" Taryn replied, forcing a smile.

"Did you cheat on him or something?" Ananya asked, ignoring Taryn's efforts.

"Huh?" Taryn scoffed. "No, I didn't. It was actually the other way around," she admitted shortly.

"Aww. You poor thing. Can I hug you?" Ananya replied with fake empathy.

"Um...okay," Taryn replied as Ananya stood up and embraced her before she could refuse.

"Are you seeing anyone yet? Or are you not ready?" Ananya asked as she released Taryn and sat back down.

"Are all your questions this personal? I've never had a table so interested in my personal life before," Taryn laughed nervously. "Would I be able to just take your order already, please?"

"Just ignore her already," Jared interrupted, leaning forward, exposing Derek who quickly ducked behind his menu. "I apologize for her inappropriateness."

"It's fine," Taryn sighed with a smile.

"See? She said it's fine," Ananya said with an attitude toward Jared. "So you seeing anyone? You seemed cozy with your friend over there," she added, turning her attention back to Taryn and pointing back over her shoulder toward Lewis.

"Yeah, we were close, but we're just friends. Like I said, I haven't seen him in almost ten years," Taryn replied. "We kinda grew up together. I'd always be at my uncle's house, and he lived next door, so we've known each other for a while."

"You lived with your uncle?" Ben questioned. "Where were your parents growing up?"

"No. My mom is one of six, and when her oldest sister had kidney failure and slipped into a coma, all the siblings would drop us kids off at my uncle's house. The older cousins would watch us while the parents went to visit my aunt in the hospital," Taryn explained. "So I kinda grew up with the people in their neighborhood, and with Lewis right next door and his dad being the one checking in on us kids, we all kinda became good friends."

"It didn't sound like they were just friends," Ananya whispered to Ben next to her.

"I'm sorry, I didn't catch that," Taryn said.

"Nothing, I just overheard them talking, and it sounded like he liked you, or you guys had a thing going on a while back," Ananya stated smugly.

"Um, we did hang out a lot, but like I said he's just an old friend," Taryn explained.

"Maybe to her, but he sounded like he sure had feelings for her," Ananya whispered to Ben again.

"I'm so sorry, I didn't catch that again?" Taryn asked.

"It's nothing. I think we're ready to order," Ananya said.

"Perfect," Taryn replied, appreciative that the drilling of questions was seemingly over. This was the strangest encounter she'd ever had waitressing.

Ananya proceeded to order for the table. She was definitely the dominant one here, while others on the table added one or two things they personally wanted to try in between. After punching the order in, Taryn left the room with a smile, happy that she could escape the random interrogation she found herself in.

*****

"Sorry I took forever," Taryn said to Lewis as she approached their table. "They just had a lot of questions."

"It's okay, Ti, your friend Chris took our order already," Tyson said.

"I'm so sorry!" She sighed.

"No, it's fine. We chillin'," Kyle said with a wink.

"So are you only up here for Nathan's grad?" Lewis asked casually.

"Yes and no. I fly back home Sunday morning. I gotta finish up the school year with my freshman," Taryn said with a smile. "Then I fly back up the first week of June for the summer."

"We fly home Friday," Kyle scoffed.

"Wait. Ti, did you say you'll be in the Bay all summer?" Lewis asked excitedly.

"Yeah! After I finished my EdD in December, I started teaching a few online courses for the University of San Francisco. A few weeks ago, they offered me a professor position to teach face-to-face summer courses up here," she explained with a smile.

"No *shit*? That's amazing, Ti!" Tyson exclaimed.

"What courses are you teaching?" A sly smile spread across Lewis's face.

Tyson and Kyle, beaming, were waiting for her response.

"Um, not sure the exact course numbers, but it's for their master's program? I'm teaching the curriculum-development course and their classroom-management course," Taryn said.

"What? Really?" Lewis laughed to himself. "Well, I guess we are going to be seeing each other a lot this summer, professor."

"Huh?" Taryn was confused.

"I'm finishing up my master's with the military stipend to be a teacher, and I'm actually signed up for the curriculum-development course, so you'll be my teacher." Lewis smiled.

"No way!" Taryn exclaimed. "Well, don't expect me to pass you just because we're friends," she joked.

"It's okay. I remember what you like. I'll be that kiss-ass student." Lewis winked.

"Suuuure," Taryn dragged as she rolled her eyes, laughing. "Well, if you need anything else just let me know. I already took care of your bill, guys."

"What?" Tyson questioned.

"It's been forever, and it was really nice seeing you guys. It was comforting." Taryn sighed. "Don't worry about it. I got you guys."

"Thank you, Ti! Love you!" Kyle said with a smile. He was never one to turn down free food.

"Everything happens for a reason, bro," Tyson whispered across to Lewis with a wink.

All Lewis could do was shake his head at the instigators sitting before him. The four of them finished up eating and precleaning the table for Taryn. They waited patiently, watching Taryn move around the restaurant so Lewis could give her a proper goodbye before the four of them left. Lewis just smiling as he watched her work.

*****

As the shift went on, tables came and went quickly for Taryn. Having the customers cook their own food in a yakiniku-style restaurant was kinda fun. Chris helped to run out the food, appetizers, and drinks to tables as Taryn continued to be Ms. Aloha, seating customers, greeting tables, and taking orders, ensuring that everyone was kept happy. The hustle and bustle of it all, keeping Taryn's mind occupied.

"Is there anything else I can get you guys?" Taryn asked Ananya's table.

"No, thank you. Everything was delicious!" Jared said.

"Okay. Well, if you guys need anything else just let me know. If not, were you guys ready for the check?" Taryn continued.

"Yes, don't need to split it. We can all just chip in cash to cover," Ananya replied.

"Perfect. I'll be right back with that," Taryn said as she turned to leave.

"Wait!" Ananya stopped her. "There is one more thing."

"What can I do for you guys?" Taryn said, turning back to the table with a smile.

"See, we have this friend who really wants to talk to you, but he thinks he messed up pretty bad already," Ben started.

"And I apologize for grilling you with questions. We wanted to see if you really were as sweet as he made you out to be. I promise I'm not typically that much of a blunt bitch. As an actress I was just playing a part to see how you would react," Ananya confessed with a look of guilt spread across her face.

Taryn was shocked and silent. Biting down on her bottom lip, the pieces began to fall into place. Actors. They're a cast here for lunch. They requested Nathan. Their "friend" thinks he messed up. This was Derek's doing.

"Hi, Derek," Taryn said to the table with a sigh.

"Hey," he replied, slowly sitting up and emerging from behind one of his castmates.

"I appreciate what you guys did here. You are concerned friends just trying to help him out. I get it," Taryn said to the table. "And, Ananya, I've been in your shoes and have done the same thing to many of the people my friends have brought into our lives, so I respect you for that. But, Derek, if you want to talk to me about something just do it. Don't cower behind your friends. And if you are going to cower, then I have nothing left to say to you," Taryn finished.

The entire table fell silent.

"I'll be back with the check," Taryn scoffed as she left.

"Fuck," Derek said, dropping his head to the table.

"Just ask her for a do-over, bro!" Ben encouraged. "Ask her on a legit date, not this 'cleaning the bathroom' shit you told us about."

"Yeah! Take her on a legit date, be romantic and woo her," Jared said.

"Show her the sweet, kindhearted guy we've all come to care for and love!" Ananya added.

"Bro, they're right. If you got any shot at fixing whatever it is you messed up, you need to do this the right way. Man up and ask her on a real date," Jared added.

Derek just sighed. He knew they were right, but how to talk to her alone was the question. If she was upset at him before, she was going to be pissed at him after this.

"Here's your check," Chris said as he approached the table.

"Where's Taryn?" Ananya asked.

"Oh, she's closing out another table and asked me to bring this over," he replied as Ananya took the check from him.

"Wait, I thought it was twenty-four dollars a person for lunch? What is all this that got subtracted?" Ananya questioned.

"Yo, shut up. Don't get mad at a discount!" Ben urged.

Ananya looked to Chris for an explanation.

"Taryn did that. She said you were friends, so she added her brother's discount to your total, so everyone only got charged sixteen dollars a person," Chris explained, before turning to walk away.

Everyone at the table was shocked at Taryn's generosity despite what they had put her through with the questioning.

"Bro, you need to fix this," Ben said to Derek.

"She is awesome. Fix it, D," Ananya added.

Derek sighed to himself. He knew he had to fix it but wasn't sure how. Looking out the door of the back room toward the main dining area, he saw Taryn at her friend Lewis's table with a huge smile on her face, as they said their goodbyes. He knew that if he didn't act fast this friend of hers would.

Ananya shared with the table the bits and pieces of what she overheard of their conversation, and it sounded like (1) Lewis was secretly in love with Taryn but was too afraid to tell her how he felt, and (2) They would be spending time together this summer as Lewis would be one of her students at USF.

As Taryn finished up her shift, she went to the back room to clean up after Derek and his castmates. On his chair, she found her bag. Pulling out the napkin tucked into the side pocket, she opened it and read, "I'm sorry. Please call me so we can talk.—Derek."

His number was scribbled and smeared in the fold. Unsure of how Taryn even felt after the embarrassment she faced with his castmates, she crumpled the napkin up and shoved it in her pocket, locked her bag in the employee break room, and proceeded to clean the restaurant. As she wiped tables and stacked dirty dishes in the bin, her mind wandered between thoughts of joy in seeing Lewis again and of her night with Derek. This would be an interesting summer.

17

Taryn

Nathan came to pick Taryn up with Reggie's car, right when her shift was about to end. His meeting had finished just in time for him to make it to the restaurant before it closed to prep for dinner.

"How was it, Ti?" Nathan asked with a smile.

"Apart from you setting me up so that Derek was here and I had to talk to him?" Taryn asked sarcastically. "It was good. I had fun. It was especially fun being grilled with questions by his castmates."

"Oh," Nathan sighed guiltily, shoving his hands in his pockets. "I didn't know his castmates would be with him, but we all wanted you guys to just talk it out. You're good for each other."

"We?" Taryn questioned.

"Yes, we. All the boys. Emma and Sienna too," Nathan stated. "Ti, I've never seen you as happy as you were last night hanging out with him—before Chase palu'd—in a long time."

"Nathan, I don't need you or your friends to be setting me up with anyone. Maybe things getting weird this morning was God's way of saying I need to be single right now," Taryn argued. "And besides, I doubt one night could have meant anything to a big shot actor."

"Well, it did," Nathan retorted.

Taryn stopped stacking clean plates and stared at her brother.

"He was a mess after you stormed out, and Emma said when his castmates went over for dinner to meet the family, all he could talk about was you. He barely even ate because he felt like such a fuck-up," Nathan continued. "Just talk to him. Please? Or I'll never hear the end of it from Emma and Sienna."

"I don't know, Nate." Taryn sighed heavily. "I'll think about it."

"Thank you," Nate said as he got up from the barstool. "I'll be outside. Just come out when you're done."

The car ride home was silent. Taryn felt exhausted. She didn't realize how much of a different energy waitressing required. It had been a long time since she had done so much consistent cardio in a six-hour time frame. She just wanted to take a long, hot shower.

Nathan pulled up to the curb of their summer apartment, and Taryn got out.

"You're not staying?" Taryn questioned.

"No, I gotta go return Reggie's car to the other apartment. Sienna's gonna meet me there to finish some more packing and cleaning, and we'll pick up Mom and Dad from their day date at the pier before we come back home," Nathan explained. "You want me to pick up dinner on our way back too? It's probably going to be late by then, that's why. Unless you wanna cook," he added.

"Sure. Some Chinese food, noodles, and dim sum preferably, sounds perfect right now." Taryn smiled through the window. "Lots of soup dumplings please!"

"Okay, you fat shit," Nathan said jokingly. "Soup dumplings and noodles it is."

As Nathan pulled away from the curb, Taryn smiled to herself. She loved her family, but they took a lot of energy that she did not have right now. She was thankful she would have a few hours alone to relax.

Dragging her feet up the stairs and turning the key on a heavy sigh, Taryn was beyond ready for a hot shower. Entering the foyer, she kicked off her shoes and placed her key on the hook that her mother had installed next to the door. The emptiness and quiet of the apartment were comforting, and she sighed to herself as she made her way to her bedroom, the coolness of the hardwood floors soothing her aching feet.

Pushing her door open, she dropped her bag onto the couch and froze in the doorway as she stared on. Pink and red rose petals were scattered about the floor with a teddy bear holding an "I'm sorry" balloon propped up in the center of the bed with a pillow.

"What the fuck?" Taryn said aloud to herself in confusion as she cautiously made her way deeper into her room.

Leaning to look into her bathroom, she gasped.

The white marble floor was now decorated with the same array of petals, with various lit candles placed all over the counter and around the tub. The tub itself was filled and brimming with bubbles and more rose petals scattered on top.

"What...the...fuck," Taryn said again to herself slowly.

Trying to take in the scene around her, Taryn was absolutely in shock. No one had ever done something like this before, and she wasn't sure if it was real or if she was hallucinating after the shift at the restaurant.

"Nathan let me in. Is it too much? It's too much, isn't it?" Derek's voice carried over her shoulder, the warmth of his breath on her neck sending a tingling sensation down her spine.

"What the?" Taryn said, spinning around startled, slipping on some petals and falling onto her behind. Panting, she clenched her chest with one hand as she stared up at him.

"Fuck," Derek said, leaning down to help her up. "I gotta remember not to do that anymore. I'm sorry. Are you okay?"

"I'm fine," Taryn said angrily, pushing his offered hand away and pulling herself up with the counter.

Derek's face dropped.

"Look, Taryn, I'm really sorry. I just—" Derek started.

"Derek, I don't need any of this crap," Taryn interrupted him. "I appreciate you taking the time out to do this for me, it is lovely. But all I needed from you is to talk. If you thought I said something you weren't sure of, just ask instead of shutting me out. Don't assume shit if you don't know," Taryn stated.

"I know, I'm sorry," Derek replied, hanging his head.

"And with that being said," Taryn continued, "I'm sorry. I shouldn't have been a hypocrite and assumed you told my parents about my divorce," she added gently, tilting his head up from the ground so he could look her in the eyes.

Derek stared into her eyes, shocked at her revelation. He understood why she was mad about the part of the conversation she walked in on, and she didn't need to apologize for that. But he thought she would be beyond pissed about his castmates interrogating her today at lunch. Appreciative that she was even talking to him, he pulled her into his chest and squeezed her to him.

"Did you draw this bath for me?" Taryn asked as her tired body melted into Derek's embrace.

"Yes, I did. And before you ask, Emma gave me the stuff and told me what to mix in so you can relax. I figured you needed it after seeing you work so hard today," Derek said as he kissed her nose.

"Thank you," Taryn replied with a grateful smile. "Wait, I thought your friend said you guys had to go back and film?"

"Ben?" Derek laughed. "He always says we're filming, but we just had a cast-bonding lunch today and were reviewing our scripts. We don't actually start filming until Monday."

"So you just came here after lunch?" Taryn asked, confused.

"No, but when you didn't text or call me after I left, I got worried," Derek confessed. "I figured you just saw my note on your bag when you cleaned our table and tossed it out. So I wanted to make a big gesture to get you talking to me again," he added sadly.

"Oh no! I'm sorry. You guys were the only table that ate in the back room, and after you left it got really busy so we closed the door to the back room, and I didn't even clean it until the end of my shift," Taryn explained.

"That's why?" Derek chuckled. "Damn, here I was thinking you and your friend Lewis hit it off, and you forgot all about me already."

"What?" Taryn said, confused. "Wait, are you jealous of Lewis?"

"If I'm being honest, yeah. He's this buff, handsome guy with nice teeth and all these sexy-looking tattoos on his arm. Ananya eavesdropped on his conversation and heard he had feelings for you in the past. Then to see him hug you the way he did…hell yeah, I was jealous," Derek said.

"You're crazy, you know that?" Taryn countered. "Lewis is just an old friend. Yeah, we had a thing before I met my ex-husband, but it wasn't serious. We just found comfort in each other, and with our history growing up together, he was a safe bet for me."

"Kinda like how we found comfort in each other the other night?" Derek said with sadness in his eyes.

Taryn scoffed. "He's just a friend, and besides, I haven't even seen him or spoken to him for over ten years. There is nothing there," she reassured him.

Derek just shrugged.

"Do you have anywhere to be?" Taryn asked randomly as she exited the bathroom and locked the door to her bedroom before coming back to stand before Derek.

Derek shook his head no.

"Well, then, are you going to make me enjoy this hot tub alone?" she asked with the sly smile.

Before Derek could answer, Taryn began pulling her clothes from her body as she walked backward to the other end of the bathroom toward the shower. Derek could feel the desire pulsing throughout his body just watching her.

"What are you doing? The bath is over here," Derek said calmly, his growing lust clear in his voice.

"I'm showering first," she said like it was obvious. "I'm sweaty, and I stink from work. I don't want to soak in my own filth." She chuckled. Taryn always showered before soaking in a tub. She never found it sanitary to just sit in the tub dirty without showering first.

"Oh?" Derek said as he walked toward her, yanking his shirt off with one hand, never losing eye contact with her.

With sunlight cracking through the small window above the tub, Derek's abs and v-cut were prominent, his muscles moving under his skin with every step he took toward her. Taryn's heart beat rapidly in her chest as her body seemed to be pulling him closer to her.

Walking backward until her back was against the cool tile, Derek's tall, lean frame blocked the entrance to the shower. With one hand he flipped on the water as droplets came tumbling down in front of them. Quickly, Derek unfastened his pants as they dropped to the floor, puddling around his ankles.

"What about Nathan and your parents?" Derek asked before taking this any further.

"Nathan's got them on a tour for a few more hours while he and Sienna finish packing all their crap at the other apartment. They'll pick my parents and dinner up on their way home," Taryn replied. "So…we have some time alone before they get here," she said with a wink.

Derek stepped out of his pants and braced himself, one hand on either side of Taryn's head as she leaned against the shower wall. Taryn's hands and eyes exploring his arms, running a trail of fire down his chest and abs. Slowly, she pulled at the elastic waistband of his boxers, and he willingly stepped out of them as they fell to the floor with his pants.

"What is with us and showers?" he chuckled.

"I don't know." Taryn laughed. "I guess scaring me until I fall onto my back in them twice has left a strong impression on me."

"Well, let's get you showered so you can soak, okay?" Derek said as he squeezed some shampoo into his hand and began to lather her hair.

"I can wash my own hair, you know?" Taryn said as she stepped closer to him, wrapping her arms around his waist.

"I know you're very independent, but would you just let me take care of you once, woman!" he replied sarcastically on a huff as he booped her nose with some soap.

"Fine. Then I'll wash you," she retorted as she lathered her washcloth with some soap and began to glide the rough material across his body.

"Ow! What is that thing?" Derek said as he flinched. "Is that made of sandpaper or something?"

"It's an exfoliating scrubber, you big baby." Taryn laughed. "It'll make your skin baby-smooth."

"Okay, that thing is definitely not sensual." Derek sighed as he rubbed his chest.

After rinsing off her shampoo, she allowed Derek to condition her hair and take his time washing her body, going the extra mile to add a shoulder massage in before scrubbing her back. Taryn was surprised by how relaxed she felt showering with Derek. The other night was simply a moment of lust that overtook the conscious thoughts of her being so intimate with a total stranger. But today it was different. She felt comforted by him being there with her, and showering with one another seemed natural.

"All clean?" Taryn finally asked as she leaned back into his chest under the water.

"Yes. You're all clean, beautiful." He sighed as he wrapped his arms around her waist and leaned down to rest his chin on her shoulder.

Taryn melted into his body with a sigh as happiness overtook her. In all her years with Toby, not once had she ever felt this way, so relaxed and connected to him. She wasn't sure if it was scary or exhilarating to be feeling this way about Derek, having known him for only a few days.

"Let's get you into the tub before it gets cold," Derek said, suddenly squeezing her body to him from behind and lifting her off her feet.

Soapsuds from the floor of the shower were kicked up as Taryn was taken off guard. Derek laughed at her reaction as she wriggled in his grasp, somehow still turning off the showerhead as he exited with her in his arms. His height made it easy for him to keep her feet from the floor.

"You're so slippery." Derek laughed as he scooped her legs up and stepped gently into the tub.

"Well, we did just come out of the shower," she said as she turned and wrapped her arms around his neck.

Slowly, Derek lowered his body into the tub, squatting down with Taryn cradled in his arms. Stretching out each leg, he turned and positioned her so she was sitting in front of him before guiding her shoulders back to rest on his chest. Taryn could feel the thud of his heartbeat in his chest as she melted into him.

"So the other night you said I could ask you five questions, right?" Derek sighed as he snaked his hands around Taryn's waist.

"Yes?" Taryn said suspiciously.

"I only got to ask one in reality, and I really do want to get to know you," Derek whispered into her ear.

"Well, I think you got to know me pretty well that night despite not getting the other four questions," Taryn teased as she pushed her behind into his groin teasingly.

"Hey, hey, hey. Stop distracting me with your awesomeness." Derek chuckled. "I'm serious. I want my other four questions."

"Okay, what do you want to know?" Taryn sighed as she wiggled from his arms, turned in the water, and leaned against the opposite end of the tub.

"Question two. Your friend Lewis seems cool. Why didn't you two end up together?" Derek sighed nervously.

"Jumping right in again, I see." Taryn sighed. "Like I said, Lewie is just a friend. I mean it was fun, I guess, but we didn't see each other as anything more."

"I call bullshit. I saw how he looked at you. There's no way you two could have been intimate with each other for so long without one of you having developed some type of feelings as more than just friends, Ti," Derek scoffed. "And if I caught feelings in twenty-four hours for you, Lewis would have to be a dumbass to not have felt anything for you after a year. He would be the world's biggest idiot."

"I guess that's true for most people, but it's not when it comes to Lewis and I. I guess at one point you could say I cared about him more than I did our other friends, but he was such a player type, I never let my feelings go beyond that. Maybe it was my way of preventing myself from false hopes that I could change him or whatever, but there were no romantic feelings. We were just friends." Taryn sighed.

"Well, even if you don't think there were feelings there, I can guarantee you that Lewis did feel something beyond just being friends," Derek retorted.

"My turn. Do you still have feelings for your ex, Lexie?" Taryn asked confidently. "It hasn't been that long ago, and just because she put you through hell, it doesn't mean those feelings simply go away."

"Why does it matter?" Derek sighed.

"It matters because I don't know what this is," Taryn said, motioning between them. "I just don't want to get hurt."

"Taryn, I would never hurt you like that. I know what it feels like, and I would kill myself if I ever caused you that type of pain." Derek leaned forward and cupped Taryn's cheek, taking the pad of his thumb and gently touching her bottom lip.

"That doesn't answer my question, D." Taryn stared at him with her dark-brown eyes, demanding an answer.

"No, I don't have feelings for her," Derek replied confidently, sitting back. "I care about her and am happy for her, but I am no longer in love with her. You can't keep loving someone who won't love you back."

Taryn leaned forward and crawled her way up his body until she was pressed up against his chest. Wrapping her arms around his neck, she got nose-to-nose with him before speaking.

"Sometimes you can't help it, though. Just please, whatever this is, try your best not to hurt me." Taryn smiled as she melted into him, his arms wrapping around her body.

"Taryn, I promise I will—" Derek started.

"No. Please don't make me any promises. Promises are too easily broken." She sighed as she rested her head on his heart.

"Okay, I'll try then." He sighed as he kissed the top of her head and squeezed her as if he never wanted to let her go.

18

Derek

They stayed, lying in each other's arms in the tub until their fingers and toes were pruned. The buzzing of Taryn's phone in her pants pocket piled in the corner pulled them back to reality. Reaching over the tub with one hand while he cradled Taryn in the other, he found her phone.

"Nathan," he said as he handed the phone to her.

"Hey, Nate," she said casually as she snuggled closer into Derek's chest.

"Head up. We twenty minutes out" Nathan said. "We got Mom guys and dinner, we should be home soon. Do you need me to grab anything else?" he emphasized slowly.

Nathan let Derek in, and he knew that he would need some time with Taryn. Asking if she needed anything else was code for did she and Derek need more time to get decent? Even if they were years apart, they were still able to have each other's backs, even in the most uncomfortable situations such as this one.

"No, Nate, we're good." Taryn laughed. "Thank you, though."

"Okay. See you guys soon." Nathan chuckled as he hung up the phone.

Taryn slowly started to peel herself from Derek's body, the cold water of the tub swooshing around them.

"Come on," she said, standing up and reaching down to pull him up with her. "Let's get dried and get dressed. Unless you want to have dinner with my parents naked?"

"Hmm…that could be fun," Derek replied jokingly.

"That's disturbing," she replied sarcastically before the two of them broke out in laughter.

Drying off and throwing his clothes back on, he watched as Taryn's body walked from the bathroom. She had a persona about her that he just couldn't get enough of. He smiled to himself, thinking about how lucky he was to have had her come into his life.

After tidying up the bathroom and putting her work clothes in the hamper, he walked into the bedroom. She had her hair clipped up in a messy bun and was wearing a tank top and sweat pants. He couldn't help but stare at her as she wiped off her makeup, revealing her true beauty beneath.

"What?" she asked as she looked up at him from her spot on the bedroom sofa.

"Nothing." He smiled. "You just take my breath away each time I look at you," he added with a wink.

Taryn just rolled her eyes at him. Sitting on the edge of her bed, Derek just watched her, smiling and trying to remember every inch of her face. He was falling for her hard and way faster than he could even comprehend.

They were sitting on the living room sofa together. Derek had used his next question to ask about her dissertation topic both to lighten up the mood and because he was sincerely interested in what she had researched. He didn't know what was more fascinating, the topic itself or her passion for what she did. He was in complete awe of her as she explained everything.

"We're home," Nathan announced, opening the door.

"We're here," Taryn said over her shoulder.

"Hey, D," Nathan said casually as Sienna, Tiana, and Noah trailed in behind him.

"Hey, guys," Derek replied with a smile, standing up and walking to the door to help them carry stuff in.

"Hey, Derek," Noah said sneakily as his eyes shifted between Derek and Taryn.

Derek took the box of Chinese food from Noah and carried it over to the dining room table.

"Soup dumplings?" Taryn asked as she closed her laptop and headed over to them.

"Lots of 'em," Nathan replied.

As they all sat down to eat, the conversation was light. Nathan talked about his meeting, which apparently he did end up having despite it initially being a ruse to get Taryn to cover his shift. Sienna vented over the craziness of her last final and how excited she was to start summer break. Derek and Taryn sat next to each other quietly, giggling to themselves with each glance.

"So, D, when do you start filming?" Nate asked, trying to include him in the family conversation.

"Monday, but we start dry rehearsals, running through lines on set tomorrow," he replied.

"That must be so cool, like to be on the set of a show. Is it stressful trying to remember your lines all the time?" Sienna asked.

"Sometimes, but it's like a story. Once you read the story line and start to embody your character, the lines tend to come easier," Derek explained.

"What was your backup?" Tiana asked.

"I'm sorry, I'm not sure I understand," Derek replied cautiously.

"If you didn't make it as an actor or couldn't get parts, what was your backup career?" Tiana drilled at him.

"I've always wanted to be an actor since I was a little kid, not for the fame or money, but because I found it fun to play different parts and test myself. But if it didn't pan out, I was going to go into real estate like my father, take over his business when I got older," Derek stated.

"Who's going to take over it now since you're acting career is taking off?" Noah asked.

"I actually have my real estate license. It was mandatory for me to get if I wanted my dad's support of my acting. But Emma is actually taking over the family business when my dad retires," Derek replied. "That's why she's moving down to LA with Reggie. She's starting in marketing, developing those skills so she can be better at selling properties to clients. When the time is right, she's going to get her real estate license and switch over to market and sell houses with my dad."

"It must be so competitive, though, to sell homes in LA?" Sienna thought aloud.

"It is, but my dad has been doing it for so long, he's established a steady client list and gets recommendations from them as well. So he's done all right for himself," Derek noted.

"So what is this?" Tiana said bluntly as she pointed a finger back and forth between Derek and Taryn.

The forwardness of her mom's comment shocked Taryn, making the soup from her dumpling squirt across the table as she tried to keep herself from choking.

"Mom!" Taryn said with wide eyes, embarrassed. "We're just friends."

"Please," Tiana scoffed. "We're not stupid. So again, what is this?" she said, motioning between the two of them.

Derek didn't know what to say, but the anguish spreading across Taryn's face urged him to provide her with some sort of support.

Taking a deep breath, he replied confidently, "I have feelings for your daughter."

Everyone on the table froze; all eyes turned onto Derek. Taryn's face was in complete shock at his honesty and blunt confession to her parents.

"I don't know how she feels about me, but yes. In the time that I have spent with her, I've developed feelings for her, and I'm not going to lie about it even if it's crazy since we've only known each other for two days," he continued.

"Well, that's all I needed to know, I guess," Tiana said with a gentle smile as she began eating again, unsure of what else to say.

"Our girl here has been through a lot, and knowing her, I'm sure she's kept the majority of what she's been through a secret to prevent others from getting hurt. But even if she's tough, we're just a little extra protective over her after the year she's had," Noah explained between bites.

"After everything she's told me, you have reason to be extra protective and concerned, especially since we just met," Derek confirmed. "But I promise, I'm not going to try and push a relationship onto her or influence her feelings. I just enjoy being around her, and the more I'm around her, the more time I want to spend with her. I don't know what it is, but she makes me happy."

"She has that effect on people," Nathan explained. "No matter how irritating I find her as a sister, people are always drawn to her energy and with her big-ass heart, she would befriend every person in need if she could."

"Aww! Nate!" Taryn teased.

"Yeah, yeah. Don't enjoy it too much before I keep talking nice about you and make myself palu in my mouth," Nathan joked back.

"Seriously, though, Ti is awesome. I already have an older sister, but she's become the second sister I never knew I needed," Sienna added.

Derek sat there listening to them compliment Taryn and watching her face flush red from embarrassment. He couldn't help but smile at her, knowing firsthand how amazing she was and that everything they were saying was barely scraping the truth of her personality.

As they wrapped up dinner and began cleaning up, Derek approached Tiana and Noah, who were washing the dishes.

"Mr. and Mrs. Okata?" he started.

"Yes?" Tiana asked hesitantly.

"Can I have permission to ask your daughter on a date?" Derek continued.

"A date? Didn't you two sleep together already? Kinda backward, buddy," Noah said bluntly with a chuckle.

Nathan, Sienna, and Taryn burst out into laughter as they cleared and wiped the table. Derek was stunned and didn't know what to say.

"Uh…I just…Um…" Derek stuttered.

"I'm just pulling your leg." Noah laughed. "Yes, you can take her on a date. Take her away forever if you want. We've already had to deal with her for twenty-nine years," he teased.

"Dad!" Taryn scoffed.

"Twenty-nine years too long," Noah added, laughing.

"Thank you. I just figured I'd ask, you know, since you guys are supposed to be spending time together up here as a family this week." Derek felt like he had to explain himself.

"True, but we spend a lot of time with Taryn back home, and she gets to spend the whole summer with her brother, so it would be nice to have some extra time with Nathan before we leave," Tiana replied.

"Thanks for just dumping me off onto someone else, guys," Taryn said sarcastically.

Everyone just laughed at her together.

"Well"—Derek took a deep breath—"would you please do me the great honor of allowing me to take you on a date tomorrow?"

"Don't you have to do your dry-rehearsal thing tomorrow?" Taryn questioned.

"Yes, but it should be done by 5:00 p.m., and I can take you out on an official dinner date if that's okay with you. I can swing by around six-ish to pick you up," Derek countered. "And that way you can still spend time with your family in the morning."

"Thanks for dumping her off on us, Derek, while you work," Noah teased.

"Sorry." Derek laughed.

"Six o'clock?" Taryn asked to clarify.

"Six o'clock," Derek confirmed.

"It's a date," Taryn said with a shy smile.

"Aww!" Sienna exclaimed. "Why don't we go out to nice dinners anymore, Nathan?" she said, turning her attention to Taryn's brother.

"Because you eat like a baby dinosaur, and it's too expensive to feed you ten nice dinners in one sitting," Nathan retorted.

"Whatever!" Sienna scoffed jokingly.

"All right, let's head off to bed," Nathan said.

"Yeah, we're pooped from today. Good night, you guys," Tiana added.

"Hey, since Taryn is with us in the morning, we can go to IKEA to get some more home stuff for summertime together. We'll definitely be back in time for you to get ready," Sienna suggested.

"Sounds like a plan," Taryn replied.

"Good night, you guys. Thank you for dinner," Derek said as everyone headed to their rooms.

"I'll walk you downstairs," Taryn said to Derek as he slipped on his shoes and she grabbed her key.

"Why, thank you," he replied as he pulled her into his side and leaned down to snuggle into her neck.

"Eww, save it for the hallway with the door closed, or go back in your room," Nathan said as he entered the kitchen to grab a bottle of water.

"Sorry, Nate," Derek replied, laughing, releasing Taryn so they could walk down the stairs. "Night."

"Okay, far enough. I don't want you walking back a block by yourself at night. I got it from here," Derek said as he stopped in the cozy lobby of the apartment building.

"Didn't you hear? I'm pretty tough. I can handle myself," Taryn joked.

"Yeah, but I don't want to risk it," Derek replied, pulling her body toward his.

Wrapping his arms around her waist and squeezing, he leaned down and kissed her on the top of her head.

"Thank you for an amazing afternoon and evening, Ti. I'm glad we were able to...talk things out," he said with a wink.

"Stop, you have to have some energy for rehearsals tomorrow," Taryn said meekly as she could feel her heart rate start to pick up pace again.

She could feel Derek's muscles tense under his shirt and his cock begin to bulge in his pants against her stomach. Derek sighed with a pout as he rested his head on hers. Even if he had spent the entire afternoon and early evening with her, it still wasn't enough. It was so hard to walk away and leave her, even if it was just until tomorrow night.

"Six o'clock," he reminded her.

"Yes, six o'clock," she said, leaning back smiling.

"Here, put your number in my phone, and I'll text you as soon as I get back to my place," Derek said, unlocking his phone and handing it to her.

Taryn did as she was told and punched in her number.

"Okay, drive safe," Taryn said to him before tippy-toeing to give him a kiss on the cheek.

"I will," he whispered as he placed his mouth onto hers, his tongue slipping past her lips as their kiss began to fill with heat. Just like that his cock was rock-hard against her stomach, and her entrance began to tingle with wetness for him. Just one kiss set something on fire for the both of them that neither seemed content with; they both just wanted more.

"Okay," she said, pulling back, trying to calm her now erratic breathing. "At this rate, you'll be late for your rehearsals tomorrow," she joked.

"That wouldn't be the worst thing," Derek countered, his lips mere centimeters away from hers, his breath spreading warmth across her face.

"Derek," Taryn said seriously.

"Taryn," he replied sarcastically.

Linking her fingers behind her neck and pulling his face to hers, she looked him square in the eyes before kissing him on the nose.

"Good night," she said.

"Good night," he replied, dropping his head onto her shoulder.

As she turned to leave and walk back up the stairs, he just stared at her. What was she doing to him? The entire ride home he couldn't fully comprehend what he was feeling, but he was excited to find out. A date. She agreed to go on a date with him, and he had to make it spectacular because after everything she had been through, he wanted to give her the world and more.

Pulling into his driveway, Derek's cell phone began to ring. It was past 10:00 p.m. already, and the only people who called him this late was his family members, and only when something was terribly wrong. Without checking the caller ID, he answered hastily in a panic.

"Hello? What's going on?" He rushed down the line to the unknown caller.

"D?" The familiar voice replied, making Derek freeze in his seat, idling the car in park.

His heart sank. Although she had texted him from time to time, it was always a "Hey" that he could simply ignore. Hearing her voice again for the first time since they broke up had Derek shaken to the core.

"Derek?" Lexie's voice carried through the phone again.

"Lexie?" Derek answered.

"Hey, D. It's been a while," she said shyly. "I miss you."

Hearing those final three words was something he had dreamed of hearing her say for months after they broke up, even after her engagement. Hearing those three words before would have given him the hope he needed that she would come back to him. But actually, hearing them now just made him sick to his stomach. It was as if she had a radar that knew he was happy, and so she swooped in to ruin it. He didn't want to deal with her. Not now.

"Derek, I know it's been a while, and after what I did to you I don't deserve the time of day, but I really need to talk to you," Lexie said.

"Lexie, I have nothing to say to you," Derek finally said with a sigh. "And I'm pretty sure the supervisor you left me for wouldn't be happy knowing you're calling me in the middle of the night," he added coldly.

"I deserve that," she replied sadly. "But please, for old time's sake? I really need to talk to you."

"Okay, so talk." Derek's shock was turning into impatience.

"It can't be over the phone. I need to see you," she emphasized.

"Talking and seeing me are two different things, Lexie," Derek clarified.

"Well, it's too important to just say over the phone," she countered. "Derek, please. I'm asking as a friend. Can you please just meet me somewhere to talk? I promise it won't take more than thirty minutes," she continued to plead.

Regardless of what she had put him through, he would always have a soft spot in his heart for Lexie, and hearing her so desperate to talk with him face-to-face made his heart ache. Even if she had hurt him badly, he couldn't be a jerk and turn his back on her when it sounded like she really needed a friend.

"All right." Derek sighed. "But not tonight. I have to be on set early tomorrow for rehearsals."

"Okay. Can I come to your set? Around whatever time you're supposed to finish? I'm asking you to let me talk to you. I can drive to wherever you are," Lexie tried to compromise.

"Does it have to be tomorrow?" Derek asked.

"The sooner the better," Lexie replied.

"I don't know, Lexie. I'm supposed to be rehearsing until five, and I have plans after," Derek said.

"This can't wait though, Derek, please," she began to beg. "Are you guys going to be rehearsing where you film? The warehouses near the pier out by North Beach?"

"How did you know that?" Derek questioned.

"Even if you don't return texts, Derek, I've kept tabs on you. Asked a few of my friends that do the social media marketing of the new shows on Netflix about your show, and they spilled where you were filming," Lexie explained.

"You been asking around about me? Keeping 'tabs' on me? What the hell, Lexie?" Derek exclaimed.

"D, just because we're not together it doesn't mean I don't care and can't support your career," Lexie said sarcastically.

"Whatever, Lexie. That's still weird, stalker-ish even," Derek replied.

"Stalker-ish or caring, it's in the eyes of the beholder," Lexie countered.

"Look, Lexie. Like I said, I can't tomorrow. After I get my full rehearsal and shooting schedule tomorrow, I'll let you know when I'm free. Maybe we can grab coffee next weekend," Derek tried to compromise.

"It has to be before the weekend, Derek! Stop trying to blow me off!" Lexie argued.

"I'm not blowing you off. You blew me off if anything when you left me for your supervisor. You're lucky I'm even willing to talk to you now!" Derek seethed.

Lexie grew quiet on the end of the line.

"If whatever you had to talk about to me was so important, you wouldn't have waited until the last minute to call. So if you can't say it over the phone now, I'm done. Have a good life, Lexie. Goodbye," Derek said as he pulled the phone from his ear.

"Derek! Don't you ha—" Lexie's voice screamed through the speaker as Derek tapped the hang-up button on his phone.

Why? Why now was she calling him? What was so important that she had to talk about that made her call him at ten at night? What was so important that she had to talk to him now? Even if they were no longer together, she was giving him stress, and he was beyond frustrated.

"Fuck!" he screamed into his car as he clenched his steering wheel before slamming his fist onto his dashboard.

Looking at his phone, frustrated by the conversation he had just had, he turned it off in a rage before Lexie could try calling back. Derek quickly got out of his car after pulling into his garage. Throwing his phone into his backpack on the passenger seat floor, he got out, locked the car, and ran up the stairs. Once inside his apartment, he threw his bag on the ground and rushed to change into his running clothes.

As he bolted down the stairs to take much-needed laps around the block, his thoughts of Lexie made his anger inside grow. Losing track of time, he circled block after block, shoes pounding into the pavement, his breath heavy with rage, sweat dripping from him despite the cold nip of the San Francisco night air. Reaching a bench at the park, almost fifteen blocks from his apartment, he collapsed onto it. He dropped his face into his hands and began to sob. He had been so happy with Taryn these past few days, but one call from Lexie blew his happiness to bits.

What did that mean, though? Was he not ready to move on with his life yet? How could Lexie still have so much control over his emotions after all this time? His thoughts were beginning to frustrate him more, and he just had to run again, so he began his journey back home. Breathing heavy, he could see the heat of his breath colliding with the cold night air. His legs were burning as he now ran uphill to get home. But he pushed himself even harder, hoping he would be so exhausted when he got back to his apartment that he would collapse and fall asleep with his mind too exhausted to think about anything.

His running paid off. As he opened the door to his apartment, the clock on his microwave read 12:07. He had been running for almost two hours. After taking a quick shower, he threw himself on his bed and let his exhaustion take him.

19

Taryn

Checking her phone, she saw 11:15 p.m. flashed on her screen. Derek had left their apartment around nine forty. Living just a few blocks away, he should have only taken less than ten minutes tops to get home. Taryn wasn't sure to be worried or not. San Francisco drivers were a little crazy, but it was late and not many people were out on the road at this time. Most people were already home, trying to get the best street parking for the night. If anything, the only cars on the road would be Uber and Lyft drivers. Walking over and knocking on Nathan's door, he opened it with sleepy eyes.

"What's up, Ti?" he said tiredly.

"Can I have Emma's number please?" Taryn asked. "It's been over an hour since Derek left, and he hasn't texted me yet to say he had gotten home safely."

"Ti, I'm sure he's fine. He's not Toby," Nathan replied, trying to comfort his sister.

But it wasn't comforting at all. Her mind flashed back to Toby constantly complaining about having to call her when he was on his way home from a night out with the boys. She only asked that of him, so she knew when he'd be on the road. The one time he didn't text her that he was coming home was the one time he drove his car into a cement wall. Needless to say, it scarred her.

"Nate, please," she replied.

"All right." He sighed as he walked into the room, grabbed his phone off the nightstand, and began scrolling through his phone to find Emma's contact. "There, just shared it with you. It should be in your text messages."

"Thank you, Nate. I got it," Taryn said gratefully as she walked back to her room. Unsure if she was still awake or not, Taryn texted Emma.

"Hey, Emma. Sorry it's so late. It's Taryn. Are you awake?" (Taryn)

"Hey Ti! I'm awake. Reggie and I are doing some last-minute packing before we road-trip-it down to LA tomorrow. You okay?" (Emma)

"I'm fine. I was just wondering if Derek was okay. He left our place around 9:40 and I just want to make sure he got home okay. I haven't heard from him yet even if he said he'd call." (Taryn)

"That's really strange. Hold on. Let me try call him." (Emma)

"He's not answering." (Emma)

"Shucks. Okay. Thank you for trying." (Taryn)

"Don't worry too much Ti. He's always forgetting to charge his phone so it might just be dead. It went straight to voice mail that's why." (Emma)

"Okay, thanks Emma. I appreciate it." (Taryn)

"Just shared Derek's contact information with you. Maybe he'll answer if you call him. Good luck." (Emma)

"Thank you Emma. Have a good night. Don't stay up packing too late or you guys are going to be too tired to drive." (Taryn)

"We won't. Good night. Oh, and Ti?" (Emma)

"Yes?" (Taryn)

"I'm REALLY happy you and Derek are hitting it off. You've been the best thing that's come into his life other than our family." (Emma)

"Aww. Thank you Emma. I'm happy we're hitting it off too." (Taryn)

"Night." (Emma)

"Good night." (Taryn)

She's probably right. His phone is just dead, Taryn thought to herself as she saved Derek's contact into her phone. *Maybe I should just text him to let him know I was thinking about him?* Before she could talk herself out of it, she opened up a new iMessage window on her phone.

"Hey Derek. Got your number from Emma. Didn't hear from you so just hoping you got home safely. Thank you for everything today. I'm looking forward to tomorrow. Good night." (Taryn)

With that, she plugged her phone in and put it down on the nightstand to charge. Grabbing the teddy bear Derek had bought her, she placed it on her nightstand and smiled as she looked at it. As her eyes drifted to her bathroom, she could see the once-beautiful rose petals, still scattered, but now wilted and beginning to brown. Her mind began to the amazing afternoon she had spent with Derek as thoughts of him caressing the inside of her made her desire to be with him again grow. Remembering the feeling of their bodies intertwined, sleep began to take her.

*****

Beep beep beep beep beep.

Taryn's alarm began to go off. Rolling over and hitting the snooze button, blue numbers reading *8:00* flashed in her face. Turning onto her back, she sighed as she smiled up to the ceiling, thinking about Derek, butterflies fluttering around in her stomach for the first time in ages. She felt like a teenage girl in a relationship for the first time again. She laughed at herself at how silly it all seemed. But Taryn couldn't help what she was feeling for Derek.

Her thoughts were slowly becoming consumed by him. Other than his looks and rock-solid body, his personality was endearing. He was so kind and down to earth despite being an actor on the verge of fame. Family was important to him, and he was such a great listener, truly trying to understand and absorb every conversation they had. He was truly a much-needed blessing in her life.

Checking her phone, she saw that there was still no word from Derek. It was eight o'clock already. He was probably at rehearsals with his phone in his trailer. *It's okay*, Taryn thought to herself, smiling and counting down until their date later that evening.

She meandered around her room, brushing her teeth and getting ready in between picking up all the rose petals that were now lying dead all over her floor. She could hear her parents already in the kitchen cooking breakfast. They were going to all head to IKEA today, which was about a two-hour drive from the city, but Taryn was excited. She had only been to IKEA once, when they first moved Nathan up here for college, and they didn't have an IKEA back home. Taryn was ready to go crazy buying all the cool gadgets and stuff she saw the last time for their apartment.

"Good morning," Tiana said as Taryn opened the door of her room. The smell of bacon and eggs rushed up her nose.

"Good morning," Taryn replied.

"Good morning," Nathan and Sienna echoed as they emerged from their room as well.

"Long drive today to IKEA. Gotta leave soon," Noah reminded them.

Standing around the kitchen island, the family quickly ate their breakfast. Taryn quickly packed the leftovers in a plastic container and put them in the fridge while Nathan began stacking the dirty dishes in the dishwasher.

"You have to wash them, Nathan," Tiana scolded.

"That's what the dishwasher is for," Nathan said, laughing, teasing his mom as he blocked her with his behind and began the cycle.

"Huh!" She scoffed as she walked toward the door.

"Let's go!" Noah said as the family followed suit, heading down the stairs and piling into Sienna's car.

Though the drive was long, the mountain scenery was absolutely stunning. It still amazed Taryn that within a short distance's drive outside of the city the scenery could change so rapidly. First, you were surrounded by tall buildings, then you have quaint houses, and suddenly you have straight nature with mountains, tall trees, and a huge lake that you can't see across to the other end.

Eventually, they pulled into the large parking lot at IKEA. The big blue and yellow signs standing out in the sky from what seemed like a mile away.

"We're here!" Tiana exclaimed. "Ti, don't go too crazy all right. Everything has to fit in the trunk."

"Well, luckily, we don't need to buy any furniture so that should save a lot of space already," Taryn replied sarcastically.

The family headed into the store and began browsing down the aisles. Taryn and Sienna found themselves drifting toward the kitchen accessories, finding a cute wine-bottle stand with an electronic cork opener and some fancy dishes and cups that looked like glass but were actually hard plastic. Sienna came across cute coffee mugs with different gold lettering on them. They ended up getting three mugs: a *T*, a *N*, and an *S*, one mug for each of them.

"Since you and Derek are getting pretty close already within a couple of days, I'm pretty sure you'll get closer once you're here for two months," Sienna stated. "Do you want to grab a *D* mug for him?"

"Umm, I don't know. That's kind of rushing and jinxing it, don't you think? Like we don't even know what we are, and I'm not even sure I would call what we're doing 'dating,' so is getting him his own mug to use at our apartment appropriate?" Taryn questioned.

She really wasn't sure. It wasn't that she couldn't afford to get him his own mug; it just seemed too "official" too soon.

"Come on, Ti, it's just a mug. Besides, you wouldn't want him to feel left out if he stays over one night and then sees us all with our matching mugs in the morning," Sienna persuaded.

"I guess you're right." Taryn sighed as she searched the shelf for a mug with a *D* on it.

Placing it in their basket, they continued their way through the store. Thinking of Derek staying over and imagining going on more dates with him, she smiled to herself. The buzzing of her phone pulled her from her thoughts as she reached into her bag to check it.

"Derek?" Sienna asked slyly with a smile.

"No," Taryn said, looking down to see that she got a new text message from a number she hasn't saved in her phone yet. "I haven't heard from him since he went home last night." She sighed.

"Don't worry. Derek's an actor, and he's on set today, so it's probably just a hectic first day for him," Sienna soothed.

Unlocking her phone, Taryn nodded her agreement to Sienna as she trailed behind her toward the bathroom department. Seeing Nathan, Tiana, and Noah, Sienna's pace hastened excitedly toward them.

Who is this? Taryn thought as she opened her iMessage app and stared at the unfamiliar number. It didn't even have a Hawai'i area code, so she was unsure of who from another state even had her number. The only people with out-of-state numbers that contacted her was her best friend who moved to Hawai'i from Texas and other teachers at her school who were with the Teach for America program. But she hadn't given her number to anyone lately, and no one she knew would just give her number out at random. Opening the text, she stared at her screen.

"Hey Ti! It's Lewis. It was nice seeing you yesterday." (Lewis)

With everything that happened with Derek yesterday, running into Lewis completely slipped her mind. She was surprised he didn't have his Hawai'i 808 number anymore.

"Hey! It was nice seeing you. Didn't recognize your number though. You finally went to the dark side I see with your CA number." (Taryn)

"Lol. Yes, I went to the dark side. Thought I would keep that 808 forever, but after splitting from Kam's mom I needed a fresh start. It was just too much drama with her family so now only Kam's mom has my number. But, I'll always be an Ewa boy at heart." (Lewis)

"Ha! You spent the latter half of life growing up in Mililani. You can't claim Ewa for the street cred anymore. Lol. On a serious note though, sorry to hear about you and Kam's mom." (Taryn)

"Ouch! Lol. Sorry eh Waianae girl. Damn, CA made me soft. I can't even hang with you no more." (Lewis)

"Lol." (Taryn)

"Well, speaking of Kam's mom I think we should catch up." (Lewis)

"Guarantee." (Taryn)

"I know you probably busy this week, so how about dinner the week you get back to the Bay? Lol. I could use a night out myself, somewhere that doesn't have a kids menu or chicken nuggets as an actual meal." (Lewis)

"Hey! Chicken nuggets are fire. Lol. Don't even play. But yeah, when I get back sounds good. I'll be sure to hit you up once I get back." (Taryn)

"Unless I just see you in class first Professor. Lol. Is it considered bribing you for a better grade if your student pays for dinner?" (Lewis)

"Omg. Shut up! You're so dumb. Lol. Don't you start calling me Professor just yet." (Taryn)

"Too late. Already changed your name to Professor Beautiful in my contacts. Lol." (Lewis)

"Vomit. Lol. So ugly that name. But I promise to hit you up when I get back okay?" (Taryn)

"Sounds good. Looking forward to it Ti. Shoots." (Lewis)

"Shoots." (Taryn)

Taryn kept her phone in her hand as they continued around IKEA. Nathan and Sienna grabbed some floor mats for their bathroom and a metal shower shelf to organize their soaps. In the bedding department, Taryn found a beautiful soft-knit throw blanket that she immediately grabbed. She could see herself snuggled up in it on her balcony at night, reading a good book with a nice cup of hot chocolate.

"I'm shocked. You guys didn't do too much damage," Tiana mocked, looking at their basket.

"It's because Ti over here bought out the entire Target store the other day, that's why!" Nathan teased.

"No, I didn't," Taryn scoffed sarcastically before pausing. "Yes, I did," she finally confessed.

The family broke out in laughter as they started loading their items onto the checkout counter. Taryn pushed past her family and covered the credit card pad with her hand before anyone else could pay. Looking at her family she knew they had their flaws, but they fit perfectly for her, and in that moment her appreciation for them was apparent. So she paid for the IKEA till before anyone else could.

"Stop that!" Tiana scolded. "We're the parents, let us do this for you guys."

"What?" Taryn teased. "Sorry, I can't hear you."

"Taryn!" Tiana snapped.

"Too late," Taryn replied as she swiped her debit card and typed in her pin. "I love you guys too."

"Thank you, Ti," Nathan and Sienna said in unison.

"*Humph*! Stubborn girl!" Tiana raged.

"She is your daughter," Noah teased as he put a loving arm around his wife's shoulder.

They all began laughing again at that as they headed out the door. Taryn truly was Tiana's daughter. Their caring yet stubborn and strong personalities were practically identical as was their passion for teaching.

"Shit, we gotta get you home, Ti. It's two o'clock already," Sienna said, checking her watch.

"Damn you women! Taking forever and a half shopping," Nathan scoffed.

"Maybe we wouldn't have been so long if you didn't take an hour to decide whether or not you wanted the chrome shower stand or the bronze one," Sienna retorted.

"She's got a point there, Nate." Taryn laughed as they put the bags in the trunk and got into the car.

"Whatever," Nathan scoffed, starting the engine and pulling out of the parking lot.

Still in her hand, Taryn's phone went off again. It was another text message. This time, she smiled at Derek's name popping up on her screen.

"Ti, it's Derek. I'm so sorry I didn't text you last night. My phone died. I'm on a short break now in my trailer so I'm only turning it on now and got to see your message." (Derek)

"It's okay. Are we still on for tonight?" (Taryn)

"Definitely, but I might be running a little late over here. We did so good with rehearsing the first few scenes this morning, they want to shoot them already while everyone's still on their game." (Derek)

"If you've gotta work, it's okay. We can always reschedule. It's not a big deal." (Taryn)

"It's a big deal to me. It's the only thing that's been getting me through today was knowing I'd see you tonight." (Derek)

"You can't help if you have to work though Derek." (Taryn)

"What if you got ready and meet me here? I'll pay for an Uber to pick you up and bring you to me here in North Beach." (Derek)

"You want me to go to your set?" (Taryn)

"Yes. We should be done shooting around 6 or 7. You can hang in my trailer while I finish shooting, I can shower in there and we can go to dinner from set." (Derek)

"Idk D." (Taryn)

"Please. I have to see you tonight. I miss you already." (Derek)

"Okay." (Taryn)

"Perfect! I already put your name on the list with our security and they know you're coming. I'll keep my phone on me and be sure to order you an Uber around 6 so be ready still." (Derek)

"Wait, you already planned this didn't you? Lol." (Taryn)

"Yes I did. Lol. The second I found out we were starting filming already this morning." (Taryn)

"Lol. Sneaky guy. " (Taryn)

"I like to call it endearing and adorable." (Derek)

"All right. Lol. See you tonight." (Taryn)

Back at the apartment, they headed up the stairs with their IKEA finds and began putting everything away. Once settled, Taryn's family all migrated to their rooms to take an afternoon nap, leaving Taryn to get ready for her date with Derek. Her excitement grew with each passing moment. After taking a quick shower, she spent time drying and curling her hair before applying a little makeup.

Using Uber Eats, she ordered a nice Italian dinner to be delivered to the apartment just before she was about to leave. That way, the only thing her family had to do while she was gone was head out for some crepes. As everyone was still napping, Taryn left a little handwritten note telling them good night and that she loved them, leaving it with the dinner that was delivered on the kitchen island.

A notification on her phone alerted her that her Uber was here. Heading down the stairs and into the car, she smiled happily as a black Hyundai Sonata pulled up to the curb, the driver rolling down the passenger window.

"Good evening, ma'am. Whoever you are meeting is a lucky person. You look absolutely breathtaking, and you smell wonderful too!" the driver noted to her with a kind smile among his graying beard hairs.

"Thank you," Taryn said, smiling to herself.

She enjoyed the rest of the car ride in silence. Soft jazz playing from the car's stereo system. Her heart seemed to match the beat of the saxophone inflections. She stared out the window as the city's lights passed her in a blur, and before she knew it, they were pulling up to a gated warehouse area in North Beach.

"Thank you, sir," she said as she got out of the Uber. Staring up at the guard shack, she felt giddy. She was about to go on an official date with Derek, and it was the first date she had been on in years. She was ready to get this night started.

20

Taryn

"Good evening. Name?" an unusually tall and bulky man asked her in a deep, scruffy voice.

"Taryn. I'm here to meet Derek Bennett?" she replied.

"Oh. You're D's girl. I'll have someone come by and drive you to his trailer," the security guard said as he barked orders down a walkie-talkie to send a cart to the front.

"Thank you," Taryn said meekly.

"You're from Hawai'i, right?" the security guard asked, trying to pass the time as they waited for the cart.

"I am," Taryn exclaimed. "Derek told you?"

"You're all Derek's been talking about since he came back from his sister's graduation. Anyone who is willing to listen he'll tell them all about you," the security guard replied. "Hawai'i, huh? I went there once. Loved their little chocolate-covered nuts that you guys are famous for."

"Macadamia nuts?" Taryn inquired.

"Yeah! Those are the ones!" the security guard exclaimed, putting a name to the nut.

"Here," Taryn said, digging into her purse and pulling out a handful of assorted, individually wrapped Macadamias and handing them to the security guard.

"Seriously?" he questioned. Taryn didn't know if he was surprised because she was offering him the candy, or if he just thought all Hawai'i people carried these around everywhere they went. For a scary-looking security guard, he was suddenly acting like a scared puppy.

"Yes," she said, opening his hand and placing the candies in his palm. "I just so happen to carry these around when I'm far from home to give to people as a small token of appreciation when they are kind to me," she said with a smile.

The security guard looked at her in shock.

"It's a tradition from my Japanese background called omiyage," she explained. "When you travel far, you bring something from home to share with new friends you make. Then, before you go back home, you find gifts from your travels to bring with you that you share with your family."

"Omiyage?" the security guard questioned.

"Yes, omiyage," Taryn said. "Try them. The brown wrapper is plain, milk-chocolate covered. The orange has the macadamia nuts chopped finely mixed into caramel and covered in chocolate. And the purple wrapping is chopped macadamias mixed with Rice Krispies and covered in chocolate. They're all amazing, but whichever you like best, I can bring back with me when I come back up for the summer, and Derek can bring them by when he comes to set."

"Thank you," the security guard said with sincerity. "You are too kind. That guy better not mess it up."

"Wait, what?" Taryn began to question just as a golf cart pulled up beside the guard shack.

"Have a good evening," the security guard said, waving, as another began transporting her to Derek's trailer.

"Here you are, ma'am," the other guard said with a smile.

"Thank you," Taryn said as she got off the cart and opened the door to a trailer with Derek's name on it.

Taryn had never seen the inside of an actor's trailer, and she was floored to see that it was like a mini apartment. He had a couch, a sitting area with two chairs, and a table, a sink, a fridge, a full restroom off to the back, and a vanity with a huge mirror. Even if the trailer was cozy, she felt awkward and uncomfortable, as if she didn't belong there.

Going to use the restroom, she suddenly heard voices outside the back of the trailer. Cracking the window in the bathroom, Derek's voice and the voice of a younger woman carried into her ears, but she couldn't really make out the conversation. Standing on the toilet, she peered over the ledge to see Derek standing with a beautiful woman with long blond hair. This woman was not one of the castmates that were at lunch with him the other day. Taryn would've remembered those golden locks and her sparkling blue eyes.

"Come on D, how could you be mad at me?" the woman said as she pouted.

Derek's hands were shoved in his pockets as her arms were locked around his waist. With a heavy sigh, he rested his arm on her shoulders as he cupped her face gently with his hands before leaning closer and whispering something softly to face. Taryn's heart began to throb in her chest. The more they interacted, the more she was sure that this was the girl he claimed to be his ex. But Taryn didn't want to assume, so she watched on regardless if she felt wrong for spying, yet unable to pull herself from the window.

Suddenly, the blond tiptoed up and mashed her mouth onto his. Instead of pushing her away, he pulled her in closer. His arms instinctively wrapping around her waist, closing the space between them altogether.

"Yeah, definitely not a castmate. They would've been saving that for onscreen, right?" Taryn questioned aloud to herself as she turned away from the window.

Taryn's breathing became erratic, her heart clenching in her chest, and her eyes were beginning to burn from the tears forming. She knew this was all too good to be true. Having to get out of there, Taryn rushed out of the bathroom and yanked her bag up from the couch. Her things went crashing to the floor. Her ziplock bag of candies that had just made the security guard so happy, spilling all over the floor. Quickly sweeping everything back into her bag, she rushed to escape from the tiny trailer that was suddenly confining her. Pushing the door open, hugging her bag to her, she ran toward the exit of the warehouses.

"Ms. Taryn?" the security guard called after her, concerned, as she blew past the guard shack.

But she didn't stop, though. She didn't know where she was in North Beach, so she just ran until she was a few blocks over on a quiet street. Taking her phone out and ordering an Uber, she leaned against the side of a building and began sobbing.

That had to be his ex, and by the looks of it, they weren't as "over" as he had claimed they were. How could she be so stupid? It was over a year since Toby cheated on her, and she was still not okay; she was still hurting. How did she expect Derek to go through what he was and be completely over his ex? Especially when she looked like that. Taryn felt more disgusted with her ignorance than with Derek.

As she waited for her Uber, her phone began to ring in her hand. It was Derek. Unable to face him right now, she forwarded his call to voice mail. Again, it rang as Derek's name flashed on her screen and again, she forwarded him to voice mail. Dropping her head back against the building, she stared toward the sky, gasping for air. Her phone began ringing in her hand once again.

"What!?" she barked down the phone, answering.

"Taryn?" a soft male voice carried into her ears. "Are you okay?" the voice soothed, automatically stopping her and her heart in its tracks. The voice was too familiar.

Taryn's voice was lost in the silence and darkness around her as she stood there on the empty street, the buildings around her being her only friends right now. This was too much.

"Ti?" the voice, familiar—a voice she could never forget—called for her once again, pulling her back to the present. "It's me."

"Toby?" Her voice broke as she finally urged his name from her lips.

21

Derek

Walking through the maze of trailers, back toward his, Derek's arm was suddenly yanked as a tiny hand and long nails dug into him, pulling him between two trailers. As he turned to find the owner of the hand that nearly ripped his arm off, he stood in shock, coming face-to-face with Lexie.

"Dumbfounded isn't a good look on you, D," she said sarcastically as she fixed her hair and stood confidently before him.

"What are you doing here?" Derek questioned. "How did you even get on set?"

"Set pass?" she said as if he were stupid, holding up a laminated Netflix access pass that hung around her neck.

"I told you I couldn't talk today. I have somewhere to be right now," Derek said, with a frustrated sigh.

"That never stopped you before from being there for me," she said cockily. "Besides, I told you I needed to talk to you."

"That was before you cheated on me, left me, and got engaged," Derek said coldly.

Lexie just hung her head, looking up at him with puppy dog eyes.

"Fine. What do you want?" Derek uttered with a frustrated sigh, shoving his hands into his pockets.

"You," Lexie said as she wrapped her arms around him.

"What?" he said, confused. "You're engaged, Lexie, this isn't right. I refuse to be that guy," he added, cupping her face and leaning forward to look her dead in the eye, so she knew he was serious.

Before he could do or say anything else, Lexie's mouth collided with his. It had been so long since he kissed her that his cock took over his body, and his arms instinctively wrapped around her waist, pulling her closer as if to savor this moment from the past.

"You taste even better than I remember," Lexie said into his mouth.

Her voice snapped him back to reality, and visions of Taryn's face shot forward as he suddenly pushed her off him, breaking their kiss. Derek stepped back, shaking his head, trying to get some distance between the two of them.

"What is it? You want to take this into your trailer?" she said, licking her lips at him and eyeing him from head to toe like a hungry lion looking at a fresh kill.

"No, Lexie," Derek replied firmly. "I'm not interested in starting an affair with a married woman."

"One, that bulge in your pants says otherwise." Lexie pointed at Derek's crotch with wicked eyes. "And two, I'm technically not married until this weekend. So you won't be having an affair with someone's wife just yet."

"You're getting married this weekend?" Derek exclaimed in shock. "And you're here? Trying to sleep with me? What is wrong with you? What are you even thinking?"

"I'm thinking, before I am confined to one dick of the rest of my life, I wanted to celebrate being a bachelorette untraditionally and get a good fucking in one last time from the best dick I ever had" Lexie said bluntly.

Derek was shocked into silence. She was crazy. Her cheating on him was definitely a blessing in disguise.

"So are we going to do this or not?" Lexie said, crossing her arms across her chest, propping her breasts up as a means to tempt him.

"Lexie, I thought you wanted to talk about something important?" Derek tried to clarify as he began walking backward out from their hiding place between the trailers.

"This is important, and we are talking," she replied sarcastically.

"I'm sorry, Lexie. No. I can't do it. I won't do it," he emphasized.

"Come on, it's just one t—" She couldn't finish her sentence.

"Security, can you please escort her off the property, and don't let her back on," Derek interrupted as he waved a security guard making rounds on a golf cart.

"Sure thing, D," the security guard stated as he parked and patted the seat next to him for Lexie to jump in.

"Seriously, Derek? Fuck you. It's your loss," Lexie scoffed, giving his balls a scoop as she walked past him. As they drove off, she tossed a handful of other choice cuss words in his direction.

Shaking his head with a sigh, he tried to process what just happened. He couldn't believe she just showed up. Walking up the stairs to his trailer, he noticed that the door was cracked open.

"What the?" he said out loud to himself. "Fucking Lexie. She must have looked for me here first."

Opening the door, he saw that his trailer seemed to have everything in its place. It was just missing Taryn. He sat down and decided to wait a bit; maybe she was just walking around the set, looking at stuff. Being on the set of a show was pretty intimidating if you've never been on a set before. So he figured he would give her some time.

Looking up at the clock hanging on the wall, the time read Six forty-five. Checking his phone, the Uber confirmed her getting dropped off here over half an hour ago, but where was she? Derek decided to call the security shack to see if she had checked in.

"Hey, Tommy. It's D. Did a Taryn check in for me?" he asked.

"Hey, yeah. She came by around six fifteen. Leon drove her to your trailer around six twenty. Derek, she is so nice! She gave me an assortment of those macadamia candies I told you about. They're so good!" Tommy began to trail off as he ate another candy from Taryn.

"Damn. Thanks, Tommy. She's not in my trailer, that's why. I thought you said Leon dropped her off here?" Derek questioned.

"Oh yeah, she left, that's why. Seemed pretty upset too." Tommy seemed to suddenly remember.

"Wait, what?" Derek began to panic. Standing up, he started pacing around his trailer, looking for any sign of her.

"Yeah, about five minutes ago, she blew past me. Looked like she was crying," Tommy shared.

"Why didn't you stop her?" Derek shouted down the phone. His foot kicked something on the ground as he neared his vanity. Bending down, he picked up a chocolate-caramel macadamia nut wrapped in orange. Staring at it in his hand, he waited for Tommy's response.

"Man, she's tiny and she runs fast! She slipped past me, and I didn't even know it was her until she was about twenty feet away. I only knew it was her because I saw her drop more candies out of her bag. I don't even think she heard me calling after her when I tried to chase her down," Tommy said. "I'm sorry, D. Is everything okay? You want me to go look for her?"

"It's okay, Tommy, I'll just call her," Derek said, hanging up and walking into the bathroom to splash some water on his face and calm down.

Suddenly, he realized why she had run. Looking up over the side of the toilet, his window was cracked open. He never left it open because he felt uncomfortable with the thought of people outside his trailer hearing him use the bathroom. His heart began to sank.

Please no, he thought to himself as he climbed up gingerly on the closed toilet seat. Looking out the window, the perfect view of where he encountered Lexie came into sight.

"Fuck," he said as he hastily climbed down from the toilet and began frantically dialing Taryn's number.

"Taryn, it's Derek. Please let me explain. Call me back."

He called over and over again, each time only able to reach her voice mail. Derek left her so many messages, he lost count.

"Please, Taryn, just talk to me. Don't shut me out. It's not what it looked like."

"Taryn, can you please call me back? I would never hurt you. I need you. Please, just talk to me."

He sent message after message, and his heart sank deeper into his chest. His head hung low, tears threatening to burst at any moment. He needed to hear her voice, see her face, and just hold her in his arms again. Seeing the clock read seven thirty, he began growing desperate and decided to send her a text.

"Taryn, I'm coming to find you. Please don't run." (Derek)

22

Derek

Derek knew she wouldn't go back to her apartment. She wouldn't face her family if she was that upset. Taryn would go somewhere where she could clear her head and take a breather. Somewhere she felt safe and calm. But she had only been in San Francisco for less than a week, and he knew there were no beaches in the area that she would go to and find comfort in.

The Spanish stairs, he thought to himself, remembering their first night together when he shared with her his spot in the city that he went to when he needed to clear his mind. It was a long shot, but it was the only thing he could think of. Derek threw his things in his backpack and rushed out of his trailer to his car. Peeling out of the lot, he zoomed past security and headed for the university.

"Please be there. Please, please, please be there," Derek repeated aloud to himself.

Within ten minutes he pulled up to the curb, turned off the car, and jumped out. His lungs burned as he sprinted up the stairs to the spot where she first kissed him as they overlooked the city lights. As he reached the top of the stairs, his heart sank as he stared at the empty opening. Taking a deep breath, he walked closer, gripping the stone balcony as he went. Suddenly, a small white envelope caught his eye. As he opened it, his heart crumbled.

It was a letter from Taryn. She knew he would come here looking for her, and she was prepared. The letter read:

Dear Derek,

By the time you get this letter I'll be long gone. If I'm being honest with myself and with you, I did truly start to feel something for you in these past few days. I wasn't sure what it was exactly until I saw you with her today. In that moment I knew what I felt for you because seeing her kiss you and you return that kiss, pulling her deep into your arms where I had just been less than 24 hours ago, tore me to pieces. Derek, I began falling in love with you the second you stood over me after scaring me in the bathroom that night after the graduation. At first, I thought it was just a physical attraction to you, but soon I realized it was much more. I know I sound crazy right now since we've known each other less than a week, and it may seem cliché to say this, but the saying is true... When you know, you know. Everything just clicked into place after meeting you and I felt so safe, secure, comforted, and just happy, truly happy for the first time and those feelings never faltered. It was never even like that with Toby.

But it is not fair of me to push my feelings onto you or make you feel obligated to give me the time of day when it was obvious today you have unsorted feelings toward Lexie. I know it was her I saw you with today. I could read it all over the body language between you two. Just know that I'm not mad at you. I want you to be happy, and if you feel like something is still there between you two, I would never forgive myself if I was the reason you didn't give it another chance with her. Everyone makes mistakes, Derek, and I want you to be happy. You deserve it. Know I don't regret a single moment with you. You taught me that it is possible for me to feel love in my heart again, even after feeling broken for so long. I will always be appreciative of you for that, so thank you. I wish you the best of luck, Derek, and I will keep an eye out on social media for when your Netflix series launches. I know it will be fantastic. Thank you again for everything. Good luck.

Sincerely yours,

Taryn

Derek couldn't believe what he was reading. Questions began flooding his mind. What did she mean she would be long gone? They don't leave until Sunday. He still had time to fix this. He had to fix this. The kiss with Lexie today confirmed that he had no romantic feelings for her and that he wanted to be with Taryn.

Shoving the letter into his pocket, he ran back to his car and sped off toward her apartment. He had to talk to her, and that was the only other place in the city she could be right now. Looking at his clock, *8:20* flashed at him over and over again, reminding him that his time was running out to prove that his feelings for Taryn were real.

23

Nathan

It was eight o'clock as Nathan opened the door to the apartment for Sienna and his parents. Everyone was so full from the dinner Taryn bought them and then the crepes, that they stumbled blindly toward their rooms.

"Good night," Tiana and Noah's voice called over their shoulder.

"Night," Sienna said as she plopped down on the couch, waiting for Nathan to come to bed with her.

As Nathan hooked his keys on the door, an envelope on the edge of the kitchen island caught his eye. He didn't see it at first as the white seemed to blend in with the marble countertops. Walking over and picking it up, Nathan saw his name on the envelope.

"What the fuck?" he said, confused.

"Everything okay?" Sienna said, sitting up and looking at him with concern.

"I'm not sure," Nathan admitted as he opened the envelope and pulled out a letter.

It was in Taryn's handwriting. As Nathan read, he began to shake his head. Sienna got up off the couch and stood behind him to see what was going on.

"Oh no," Sienna said as she grabbed onto Nathan's arm, offering support.

"Fuck!" Nathan scoffed softly as he read on.

Dear Nathan,

I knew it would be you to find this letter. By the time you read this, I'll be at the airport already getting ready to board. I know it is hard, but please don't worry too much, okay? In this envelope I've updated and printed Mom and Dad's itinerary for their flight on Sunday. They've been upgraded to first class as my feeble attempt to apologize for dipping out on you guys without a proper goodbye. I just needed to go home already, and hopefully I'll be back to teach the summer courses. We'll see, but I'll keep you posted and have already wired money from my savings to Mr. Bennett so you and Sienna don't have to worry about rent for the summer.

I honestly don't know where to start. The last 8 hours alone have been a roller coaster, so please forgive me for irrationally leaving the way I did. Things with Derek aren't going to work. It isn't his fault, but I'm just not ready for whatever "it" was between us, and I think he owes it to himself to see if he still has feelings for his ex or not. Toby called too by the way. Since we ended on good terms for having gotten a divorce, I still promised to be his friend and be there if he ever needed me, and right now he does. It's not my place to say exactly what is happening with him back home, but know I wouldn't go running to his aid unless it was absolutely dire. This is something I have to do.

Again, please don't worry. Apologize to Mom and Dad for me, but I promise you I'm okay and I'll call you as soon as I touch down in Hawai'i. Love you guys. See you soon.

Taryn

"What the actual fuck?" Sienna said, eyes wide. "What did we miss during our nap and getting crepes?"

Suddenly, the buzzer went off at their door, signifying someone was outside for them. Walking over to it, Nathan waited to see whose voice came over the speaker.

"Hello? Taryn? Nathan? Is anyone home?" Derek's voice rang.

"Should we answer it?" Sienna asked.

"Not right now," Nathan replied to her. "Maybe if we ignore him, he'll go away. He knew we were going to be out tonight with Mom, then and our car is hidden in the garage, so maybe he'll just go away."

"Taryn?" Derek's voice cracked as he spoke through the speaker, as if he were on the verge of crying into the little buzzer box outside. "Please, talk to me."

"We shouldn't be listening to this," Sienna whispered, as if Derek could hear them listening from upstairs.

"If you won't talk to me now, I'll sleep in my car and wait out-side until you're ready to see me. I'm sorry. Just please know that," Derek sobbed through the speaker.

"What is he sorry for?" Nathan asked Sienna.

"I don't know. I was with you," Sienna retorted as she went over to the speaker box and muted it. "Let's just go to bed."

Walking away from the speaker box toward their room, Nathan couldn't help but feel sympathy for Derek. Whatever happened between him and Taryn that night, it seemed as if Derek truly cared for his sister. But what was Taryn thinking? What else happened tonight? And most importantly, why was she suddenly running home to Toby?

About the Author

Gianna Emiko Barnes works in education and enjoys writing in her spare time. She is the wife of an electrician and enjoys spending time with her dogs. Having been born and raised in Hawaii, she enjoys hiking, fishing, and going to beach barbecues with her family. She also loves the holidays and traveling. Gianna has a big heart, especially for her family, friends, and students, willing to go above and beyond for those she cares for.

In her writing she likes to portray strong, resilient characters who are able to overcome even the most difficult obstacles in her novels while still maintaining a sense of relatability with her readers. Her novels are set to transport her readers to a place of lies, lust, and love, keeping you at the edge of your seat around every turn. While her characters are fictional, what they go through is very real, and hopefully we can learn something from each of them.

CPSIA information can be obtained
at www.ICGtesting.com
Printed in the USA
LVHW030328060821
694612LV00002B/242